PORT LANDS

TOD MOLLOY

DEBTFORD PRESS

Copyright © 2022 by Debtford Press.

1st edition published 2022.

2nd edition published 2023.

Published simultaneously in the United States of America by Debtford Press.

Library and Archives Canada Cataloguing in Publication data is available upon request.

ISBN: 978-1-7782626-2-3 (ebook)

ISBN: 978-1-7782626-1-6 (trade paperback)

ISBN: 978-1-7782626-0-9 (hardcover)

ISBN: 978-1-7782626-3-0 (paperback)

This is a work of fiction. Names, characters, places and incidents either are the product of the author's imagination or are used fictitiously. Any resemblance to actual persons, living on dead, events, or locales is entirely coincidental.

Public domain images by Pamela Colman-Smith (1878-1951) used under Creative Commons licence CC-BY-SA-3.0

Cover Art by River Design

Debtford Press. 6 Belsize Drive, Suite 223, M4S 1L4, Toronto, Ontario, Canada.

www.debtfordpress.com

For J.

A real-life femme fatale.

When the dream begins, you're already falling.

PORT LANDS

XIX

WEDNESDAY

CHAPTER
ONE

The worst thing about this job is how badly I need it. Downtown we pack up condos. In the burbs we ferry clutter to the dump. Around here we evict low wage workers from rental apartments they could barely afford in the first place.

Garbage buildings always have sophisticated names. The Ambassador. The Diplomat. The Regency Arms. This morning we've been dispatched to The Metropolitan. Twenty-eight stories speckled grey in pigeon shit. Pregnant plaster ceilings. Threadbare carpets fossilized in stains. Familiar smells fermenting in the hallways, boiled fish, unwashed balls, cat piss and crack smoke and soup. I can hear every television set. Every unhinged conversation. Every obese pensioner coughing up a lung.

The legal text is a formality but John likes to read it out loud. Tracing his index finger across the page. Plodding through each sentence in his dopey bass boat drawl. When he's done he spits tobacco juice into a paper cup he keeps folded in the pocket of his shirt.

"I ain't leaving yet you big dumb fuck," the lady hollers from behind the wall.

He's about to call her a cunt. I can tell by his posture. Chest pushed out. Forearms bulging. Tobacco lumped inside his cheek. John despises these people. He's two missed pays from being one of them.

The door cracks open. Smoke billows out in a stale grey plume, swirling in a haze around his face. He stifles a cough, fanning with the paperwork, cheeks flushed hot bright red. Then he clears his throat and starts from the beginning, this time shouting every word.

The lady lunges out into the corridor. "You can't kick me out till I buy my groceries, that's the law. You hear me captain fuckface? That's the goddamn law right there."

"Groceries," he mutters, smoothing out his shirt. "How can YOU afford groceries you sad old cunt?"

Deep foreboding silence seems to pressurize the hallway. Neighbouring deadbolts slide into locked positions. I hold my breath hoping for violence and the afternoon off.

The lady rocks back on her heels and musters up a cough. Then she cranes her neck and spits with everything she's got. John ducks an instant too late. The pearly yellow wad hits him dead in the face. He claps his hand over his eye and tumbles hard into the wall. The lady grunts and slams the door. I stand back and watch from down the hall. I don't get paid to talk.

John struggles to his feet. He tucks in his shirt and re-packs his dip and saunters slowly up the hallway, emasculated, scraping mucus off his face and wiping his hands with the eviction notice. He brushes past and rattles the elevator button, avoiding my gaze.

"We may as well take lunch."

CHAPTER
TWO

I t's too cold to sit outside so we eat together in the truck. John slurps lukewarm ravioli from a brown and beige thermos. Kev comes back from the store munching ketchup flavoured chips. John listens to sports talk radio and chews with his mouth open. Kev pulls his hood over his face and falls asleep against the window. I eat my peanut butter sandwich in silence, dreading the grainy crackle of John's speakerphone.

In a minute John will call his best friend, Dale. John will complain about cyclists and low quality officiating in major junior hockey. Dale will boast about his second cousin, Big Lou.

Big Lou might be switching to a plant based diet.

Big Lou's bathrooms have in-floor heat.

Big Lou's truck gets best-in-class mileage.

Big Lou's ex-wife has huge fake tits.

I'M SMOKING a joint behind the dumpsters when I spot a dead raccoon lying paws up in the gutter. Eyes rolled back.

Shrivelled grey tongue caught between its teeth. Bloated and filthy like some kid's forgotten toy.

There's a whooshing sound overhead. A crow swoops down and lands on the concrete, circling the carcass, pecking and prodding with its beak. Then it cocks its head and slowly turns around. As if it knows I'm watching. Round black eyes, monstrous and opaque. Glaring back at me with palpable intent.

The lady shuffles past us on the sidewalk. She doesn't notice the strangeness of our confrontation. She doesn't look at us at all. And I start to wonder if the crow is even real. If it might be a clone or a robot. If it knows who I am.

The crow is first to blink. It bends and rips a gash across the raccoon's belly. Purple-red guts dribble out in a loose wet bundle. It shoves its beak into the entrails, rooting through the rancid innards, plucking out the organs and choking them down its gullet.

I back away, nauseous. Tired of the bird's sick game. But the crow carries on unfettered. Crimson stain spreading slowly up its beak. Holding my gaze as it tears the corpse to shreds.

The lady stops near the truck to light a cigarette. Black hightop sneakers. Limp white leggings. Faded pink jacket with fake fur trim. She sets her groceries on the ground and cups her hands around her lighter. She takes two quick hauls and blows the smoke out sideways from the corner of her mouth.

John's still hunched behind the wheel watching videos on his phone. Snowmobile racing highlights. Bikini babes driving bulldozers. Ten rich families who control the world. He lowers the window and points at Kev.

"You try fucking talking to her."

The building manager waddles outside frowning and buttoning his coat. He spots me near the dumpsters and trudges across the lawn, propelled by inertia and a lust for small talk.

"Told you this would happen," he says, stomping snow off his boots. "These people. Fucking degenerates. If you can't pay, you can't stay. Am I right buddy?" I try and remember his name. Vic? Sid? It doesn't matter. Silver hair. Sausage fingers. Stout and sturdy like a pumpkin. "When did the city get so fucked?" He points at the gridlocked cars crawling south toward the Gardiner. "I'll never get home. I've spent three hours stuck in traffic this week and it's only Wednesday."

I shrug and mumble out some bullshit normally reserved for elevators. A joke comparing traffic, weather and the Maple Leafs. Vic roars with halitosis-laden laughter. Breathing in volatile spurts, huge gut shuddering beneath his coat. He slaps me on the back and socks me in the shoulder. Now we're pals.

I nod toward the others. "Watch this."

Kev engages her methodically, feigning shyness. Eyes pre-moistened. Hands clasped tightly to his chest. He's not a smoker but he offers her a cigarette and even lights it for her. Leading with empathy. Making her feel seen and heard. Putting on a real fucking show.

"Little shrimp's got a gift," Vic snorts. "Where'd he pick this up?"

"Dating websites. Reality television. Juvenile detention centres."

"Better him than me. This one, let me tell ya buddy, she's a real piece of work. Can't say I'll miss dealing with her bullshit every goddamn day of the week. This one time—"

Vic gets interrupted by groceries hitting pavement. The lady's gone berserk. Kev retreats, palms raised in mock surrender. But there's no stopping her now. Immigrants.

Banks. Vaccines. Liberals. A true believer, convinced the ideas are her own.

"You guys get many calls like this?"

"Since Christmas, maybe two or three a week."

The lady paces up and down the driveway, gaunt shadow gliding over crushed tin cans and frozen dog shit. "Can't you see whats going on? I was born here. I've lived here all my life. I was born here, goddamn it, but these people," she gestures at the other buildings on the street, "these people get whatever they want."

Smoke trailing from her cigarette draws a white line through the air. Tenants wearing bathrobes emerge on balconies above us. Vic sighs and taps my elbow.

"Sit tight buddy. I'm gonna go call the cops."

CHAPTER
THREE

I found this job on the internet. A recurring post on a janky website used by local hookers and off-shore scammers selling crypto tokens and counterfeit boner medication. "Local logistics company seeks hardworking Owner/Operators. Flexible full-time hours. Competitive compensation. No experience required. Apply by phone or text message."

I didn't need a vehicle. Didn't need an address or a bank account. They didn't run a background check or ask about my credit history. They photocopied my health card and made me sign a waiver and that was it. I was hired.

We get paid by the kilometre. Then our wages get adjusted by a proprietary algorithm the company calls a "worker productivity score." Each cheque comes with a five page summary, itemized and reconciled and annotated. If I even bother with the math, my pay comes out below the minimum wage. But I'm not an employee. I'm an independent contractor. So I can't say shit. If I complain they'll fire me and the next day another desperate fuck will come and take my place.

On my first day on the job, John bought me a coffee and

took me aside. "There's only three things you need to know about this job. Number one: slow is fast. Number two: the customer is the enemy. And number three: don't fart in the truck."

WE FINISH the eviction around three. I head downstairs and grab my coat from the truck. Kev's already slouched in the cab, boots splayed on the dashboard.

The others are still inside. I watch them through the lobby window like a TV show on mute. Vic leans against the wall, slowly peeling a banana. John drums a pen against his clipboard, bobbing his head to the improvised beat, mouth half-open, bovine gaze devoid of all awareness or concern. The lady sobs gently while the cop guides her through a selection of brightly coloured pamphlets. Landlord and Tenant Board. Liberty Village Respite Centre. Coupon book for submarine sandwiches.

On the way back to the yard John will blab about big jobs and big machines and doing real work when the weather gets warmer. Kev will stare blankly at his phone, pretending to listen, swiping through photographs of strangers. John will park the truck on the sidewalk in front of the convenience store. Kev will buy two hot dogs from the plexiglass case on the counter. John will purchase cigarettes and place his bets on this week's games.

I decide to walk home. I say goodbye with nods and fist bumps. I zip my parka and pull on my toque. It starts to snow. John puts the truck in gear and drives south toward the highway. Past the cheap Swedish furniture we stacked like garbage on the boulevard. Past the ruined groceries still strewn across the driveway. Kidney beans. Powdered milk. Asphalt and road salt and slush.

I cross the street and light a joint. The lady saunters back outside. Unlit cigarette dangling from her lips. Make-up cracked and smudged around the eyes. Cotton bag held limply in her fingers, as if picking up her things will complete the one transaction she's been trying all day to avoid. Her bag is from the food bank. They give them out for free. We lock eyes and she finally recognizes my face. I lift my arm and wave. She smirks and lights her cigarette, then turns her back and walks away. I take another haul and drop the dead roach down the sewer. And the snow floats down like ashes in the empty space between us.

CHAPTER
FOUR

Queen Street West is like a patient in a coma that for decades has refused to die. Tow-truck rigs and parking cops performing afternoon duets. High school kids hanging out in greasy packs outside every fast food restaurant, impervious to common sense or calories or cold. Inexplicable retail businesses persisting like expensive practical jokes. A condom shop. A vegan butcher. A store that only sells stickers.

The line-up at the shelter stretches right around the block. Local homeless queuing to escape another vicious night outdoors. The girl with the bright green hair and the matching neon laces in her knee-high leather boots. The bird man, the opera singer, the bicycle thief. The elderly cowboy, his tasselled denim jacket and his black ten gallon hat, his baffling golden tan. All those wayward faces, recognizable yet somehow easily ignored. Congregating under highway bridges. Camping out in city parks. Faces so weathered and familiar they've become involuntary infrastructure.

I cash my weekly paycheque at the money lending spot. Put half into an envelope. Stuff what's left inside my wallet. Grab some almost legal weed from a not-so-legal clinic.

TOD MOLLOY

Duck inside a shop to pick-up milk and eggs and coffee. Head back up to Dundas and catch a streetcar heading west.

Brand new plastic streetcar. Rolling shelter for a less beleaguered cohort. Tinted panoramic windows. Antiseptic tear resistant cushions. Strangely quiet, like we're hovering above the tracks. Mattress ads laminate the inside walls in blue and mauve and lavender. Freedom Starts With A Good Night's Sleep.

The usual riders take their usual rides. Overweight frat boys compare ketogenic diets. Performative couples display their true authentic selves. Grey-faced middle managers struggle to remain conscious, pants tucked into their galoshes.

We glide further west along Dundas Street. A disembodied voice announces all the stops. Across the aisle a mousy young woman reads post-apocalyptic fiction. A sticker on the cover says it's Heather's Pick. Every time she turns a page, she licks her finger first. I watch the woman lick her finger. I think about influenza. Trace amounts of fecal matter. Tiny particles of semen. I lay my arm across the seat and watch the skyline shrink behind us. Stately banking buildings clad in ivory, black and burgundy. Projects sprouting up along the lakeshore, too many cranes to count. The latest Bloor Street monolith, enormous and still climbing skyward. And looming high above them all, peering into every window, blanketing every enclave in its totalizing shadow, an obscenity in concrete, straight and white and perfect. The Tower.

IN UNIVERSITY my dreams caught fire. Classmates studied and played sports. Toiled away at boring part-time jobs. But those banal pursuits never held my interest. I was hopelessly pre-occupied. Consumed by opulent surroundings. Seduced by multiplying wealth. Cars and clothes and real estate. Assets earning higher salaries than jobs. Hotels that were restaurants, bars that were hotels, nightclubs with casinos hidden somewhere in the back. Lecture hall discussions could simply not compete. And nothing seemed likely to quench these mad desires, except to acquiesce.

There had to be an entry to their world. A white space ripe for capture. A path to exponential growth. But ideas remained elusive and this absence burned a hole inside my brain. I stopped eating. Couldn't sleep. At night I roamed the campus grounds, catatonic. Picking fights with drunken strangers. Robbing curfew breaking teens. Stealing compact discs from shitty unlocked cars.

I was lying in the grass the night I met The Tower. Flat on my back in the centre of King's College Circle, staring upwards. Waiting for a sign.

When The Tower spoke, I listened.

When it beckoned, I obeyed.

Time passed. I did what was expected. I graduated and took a decent job downtown. I held my nose and bit my tongue. I waited for my moment and when at last that moment came, I was ruthless. I neutralized my rivals. Castrated every enemy. I strove and raged and plundered. The world incentivized audacity and I was paid in full. And throughout my storied rise, The Tower was there, coaxing me skyward, compelling me to climb. We were more than friends. We were partners. Equals.

But that was years ago and things have changed. I've become a servant, indentured by my debt. The city is a market. The Tower is a pimp. Toronto is a pyramid scheme. The only way to reach the top is to start there to begin with.

. . .

I GET off at Howard Park. It's still snowing. The sun is almost down. The cars flying past cut tracks in the slush. I step into the street, waiting for a gap in the traffic. I think about unchecked urban sprawl. I think about self-driving cars and symbolic mass castration.

A brand new jeep stops hard along the curb. The driver lowers the passenger window and leans across the seat. "DON'T STAND IN THE BIKE LANE ASSHOLE."

Crisp white shirt. Freshly shaved chest. Eyebrows waxed in a salon. Shaking his head as the window slides back up again. Shaking his head all the way home, back to the over-priced house he's been using as a bank, back to tanning beds and boner pills and secret late night burgers in the garage, back to his botox spandex wife and his spoiled shitty kids, back to sexting with his secretary while he's sitting on the toilet. Back to Oakville.

Church bells split my eardrums. The mirror breaks inside me. That good bad feeling that comes when it wants and stays till it's done. THE SURGE.

I circle the jeep and leap from the bumper to the hood. The driver locks his doors, digging in the console for his phone. I start jumping up and down, slowly at first, then landing harder and harder, until the hood craters and the engine stalls and tiny cracks snake up the windshield. He fumbles with his cellphone, shouting nonsense at his coward fingers. I hop back down and drive my elbow through the glass. The window shatters like confetti. The driver shrieks. His pants turn dark with piss. Tears roll down his glass encrusted cheeks. He's not such a tough guy anymore.

I yank out the seatbelt and wrap it twice around his neck and now he's moaning please don't please please don't and I grab his head and smash his face into the wheel and he blub-bers I'm sorry I'm sorry I have a wife and kids I'm sorry and I punch him hard in the mouth and shout, look at me, look at me, you still think you're a bad man, but we both know the answer and I put my thumbs over his eyes and push and they feel like two ripe grapes ready to burst and then he faints and his forehead's split wide open and the blood is running like a river down his face and he's slouched against the wheel in a puddle of his own pathetic piss and then it's over.

I stick my head inside the jeep. It stinks like leatherette and piss and gabardine. I take his phone and empty out his wallet and wipe my prints off anything I touched.

These people.

They just don't know what I can do.

What I'm capable of.

CHAPTER
FIVE

P eople have been watching me for weeks. I spot them on the subway. I pick them out in crowds. Businessmen. Insurance Brokers. Chartered accountants. Clandestine operatives, disguised as ordinary people, working together, stalking me. At night they tail me through pedestrian tunnels, the sound of our footsteps caroming off the concrete walls. Every time I stop walking, so do they. Encrypted messages. Co-ordinated surveillance. Tiny bird-like drones. Strange cars parked all night in front of my apartment. Plain white rental vans circling the block until I'm finished work. But I've done all this before and I know what not to do. I use a burner phone. I rent a mailbox down the street. I even changed my name. I live my life in analog. Simple. Anonymous. Safe.

I'M TOO late to avoid the crowds. Delivered by airport limousines. Striding over jauntily from nearby lofts. Wrapped in sheepskin and goose down and cashmere, choking the shops and clogging the avenues, multiplying like clones. Somehow, this is where I live.

Who are these people. Hasty sullen people, scuttling from shop to shop. Tapping toes in checkout lines draped in perfect clothing. Frantic eyes held captive inside plumped and painted sockets, conceding truths their plaster faces can't express. Eyes that say, I'll feel better when I get home. Except home is exactly the same. Home is just another frenzy. Home is a decadent ritual.

But there are still things to buy and there's only a sliver of time. Time for truffle oil and coffee pods. Artisanal soaps and grain-fed veal. Time for compounding pharmacies and bespoke charcuteries and a pre-cooked meal in a box.

Across the road paper millionaires wearing bluetooth earbuds shovel coloured concrete driveways. Bundled young heirs build fabulous front lawn snow forts. Home addresses are proclaimed to the world via polished steel numerals and custom back-lit monograms.

Further south, the snowfall thickens, floating softly in the antique yellow lamplight, dampening the shrill procession of the streetcar. The crowd thins. The faces change. Nurses and tradesmen and teachers. Decent people working normal jobs. And I envy them in a way I never dreamed possible. Jealous of their access to credit, pensions and benefits, sick days and vacation pay and modest ski trips in Vermont. But I never let it show. I can't risk being noticed. So we walk home side by side again, like we do most nights. Pre-occupied with work and money. Defending our backyards and balconies. Masquerading as allies.

FATHER'S in the lot behind the church unloading cardboard boxes from a shitty red minivan. He moves brusquely and his mood is hard to read. Pale grey eyes, wolfishly alert. Smooth red face like a farmer. Heavy boots and stiff brown pants and a worn-out leather coat. He looks older now. But he's always looked old to me.

"I heard you were in town," he says, picking up a box. "I was not sure if it was true. How long have you been back, my son?"

"Just a few weeks."

This is a lie.

I've been back for months.

"And so," he says, accent getting thicker in the dry winter air. "How does it feel to be home?"

"Colder."

He spits a glob of phlegm across the pavement. "You've lost weight, non?"

I shrug and say nothing.

"Someone told me, just the other day, that you're going by a different name?"

I change this subject. "Need a hand with those?"

"Yes," he says, deadpanning. "I want you to do them all."

Father laughs.

I force a smile.

We load the boxes onto metal carts and wheel them to a yellow kitchen that smells like burnt coffee and dish soap. Father whistles with his fingers and two boys rush into the room, pale skinny teenagers with ugly matching haircuts dressed in the flowing black gowns of the church.

Father gives instructions in stern rapid French. They nod their heads but never speak. One of them scribbles on a notepad. The other opens boxes with a knife. Father hovers nearby, assessing their work, as though the task is somehow part of their religious education. It's only later that I realize they're twins.

A toddler peeks his head into the doorway. Four, maybe

five years old. Bright blue eyes. Curly blonde hair. Corduroy pants with big folded cuffs. Father doesn't seem to notice.

The face appears again a few moments later, giggling softly. Playing peek-a-boo with the grown-ups. This time Father lunges fiercely at the door, cursing and snapping his fingers. The little boy bursts into tears and runs off down the hallway. Bare feet slapping on the cold tile floor. Fainter and fainter and then vanishing completely.

The twins finish the count. Father mulls the totals, grumbling and chewing on his pencil. Then he grunts and snaps the notepad shut and the four of us move the cargo from the carts onto the countertop. Each box weighs about ten kilos. Father never says what's inside. And I never ask.

We wheel the empty carts into the closet. The twins bow and shuffle backwards from the room. Father sighs and leans against the kitchen wall, flushed and breathless, drinking deeply from a dented metal flask. He wipes his mouth on his sleeve and leads me out into the church, gnarled fingers grazing along the wall for balance. Light filters down through the narrow stained-glass windows, distilling medieval patterns on the floor. The radio crackles to life. Brassy music fills the air, reverberating through the old stone building, collecting like vapour in the rafters. The church becomes an old speakeasy, where Father is both bartender and customer. Where business is always good.

"Have you found a place to stay?"

"Yeah, just up the street."

"And?"

"I like it so far. A big empty room is a luxury."

He sits and lays his arm across the pew. "You have something for me, no?"

I hand him the envelope. He slides it away without counting what's inside.

We sit in silence for a while. He takes a long greedy drink

from his flask, gazing up at the portrait on the wall. Cheap black plastic frame. Once bold colours faded into vague pastels. More like a poster than a painting. The young man has long dark hair with big eyes and a short flat smile. He wears a red velvet robe with a matching jewelled crown. In his left hand he holds rosary beads. In his right hand he holds flowers. Protruding strangely from his sleeve is a third hand, holding an identical bouquet of white and yellow flowers.

I sit and watch him stare. Hearing aids nestled in both his ears. Brown spots spreading on his hands. Washed up and feeble and wasted. And yet I know his failing body is a camouflage, a skin that can be shed. But I'm not here to wake any beasts. I'm here for penance. I'm here to buy myself some time. So I listen to him tell the tale of Saint Casimir, the way he's always done.

"Did you know young Casimir was a Prince? That he was a scholar and then a soldier, that he almost became a King? That he died of tuberculosis when he was just twenty-five years old? And when they opened up his tomb, one hundred and twenty years later, a magnificent fragrance filled the church and lingered there for six straight days..."

FATHER FINISHES THE STORY. Eyes half-open. Slouched over and leaning on his elbow, head resting on the pew.

"So how much do I owe you now?"

"I will have to check on that for you," he says. "One twenty? One thirty?"

"Seems like more than last time."

"C'est possible," he says, unscrewing the cap. "Inflation, interest, times are tough you know. And kids these days, they are so expensive."

He dangles the flask in front of me.

"No thanks."

He shrugs and takes another swig. "Do not be this way. It was a loan, not a gift. You know this."

"How do you expect me to be?"

"I expect you to pay your debts."

"Funny. Thought I did that already."

Suddenly the old drunk disappears. His eyes darken. His lips pull tight across his teeth. "Protection has a price," he growls. "And storage does as well. The congregation has been generous so far, but I am not equipped to clothe and feed collateral. Do you understand what I am telling you?"

I nod.

He eyes my uniform. "Maybe the time has come to stop screwing around. Let me find a job for you. Something that is worth your while. People, they still ask about you. I never know what I should say to them. I tell them you retired."

"I did."

"Yes, yes, you have said that, I know. But still, they ask." He takes another drink. "Someone came around, you know. It was just the other day. Or maybe it was last week. Anyway, they came around. They had a job for you."

My heart pounds. "What did you tell them?"

"It was a while ago," he shrugs. "To be honest, I don't remember exactly what I said."

"What kind of job?"

"The old kind, of course."

I stand up and get ready to leave.

"So what then? You work these bullshit jobs forever? How many jobs? Three? Four? Never sleep? Never take a day off? Take the job. There is no going straight, not after what you did. Take the job. Never mind what I said or who I said it to. Sit back down and have a drink. Stop worrying so much."

But I'm worried all the same.

CHAPTER
SIX

I leave him snoring on his back beneath a blanket. Kill the lights and lock the door and take the stone steps to the street. The stores are mostly empty. The restaurants are bright and full. The snow comes down in big wet flakes that turn to water when they hit the ground. It's half past seven and thanks to Father's empty flask I've got just enough time to be late.

I watch her from the streetcar stop. Behind the counter of the flower shop that used to be a convenience store. Hair pulled up in a frizzy bun. Reading glasses halfway down her face. She punches keys on the old metal cash machine, chatting with her customers, remembering their names and faces.

When we met I felt the gravity between us. A weight that couldn't be explained. Now I'm getting to know her in short daily increments, chance encounters in the overlapping spheres of our routines. She slurps her morning coffee. She smokes but only when she drinks. She likes punk rock music from the nineties and weekday trips to the zoo. She carries herself with this cool easy grace that other people often think is odd.

Sometimes she wakes me up at dawn, working briskly with her tools downstairs. Sometimes she sings along with the radio. Sometimes she hums her own made-up tune. And I listen and I wonder if she hears me too, or if she even thinks of me at all. At night the smell of her flowers wafts up through the floorboards and into my apartment and I lie awake, alone with her scents. With her queen anne's lace. With her roses and lavender.

The telephone rings. She picks up the receiver and briefly turns her face toward the street. I lift my palm and wave. My breath fogs up the glass. I use my sleeve to wipe away the moisture. And then I see a man.

He's facing my direction. Standing very still inside a doorway up the street. Ankle length coat. Black bowler hat. Tall and skinny with a narrow face and bloodless skin as white as bone. I scan the block. The streets are abandoned. For the moment we are totally alone. I look south and there's a streetcar coming. I turn back and the man is sprinting straight toward me, spindle-thin legs spidering beneath his torso, rapid stop-start movements like some hideous marionette.

The streetcar slows and stops. The man is only steps away. I rush onboard and throw myself into the seats. The red lights flash. The doors slide shut. We set out smoothly north along the tracks.

I wait as long as I can stand it. I count to five and turn around. The thin man stands motionless between the rails, watching me. Silhouette set against a darker shade of black. Gaunt face blurring as he's resorbed by the night.

CHAPTER
SEVEN

The hole was a small dank room beneath the prison. Stainless steel toilet. Stainless steel sink. Gaping black drain in the middle of the floor. Eleven weeks without a mattress. Eighty days without the sun. They confiscate your letters and your magazines and books. They rob you of your dignity, your money and your name. They turn you loose but they never set you free. Down there everyone's a congregant. Everyone's an orphan. Everyone's a child of God.

They used to let him visit once a week. He brought us carbonated drinks and chocolate bars, coffee crystals and potato chips. He passed out cheap brown bibles and recruited inmates to his Christian studies program. It was twelve weeks long and if you attended every session you got a nice white bible with a golden crucifix embossed on the cover. The other guys would carry them around like born again rappers or made-for-tv minstrels. Later they would trade them for pills or trace the cover onto wax paper and use it as a stencil for a dip and poke tattoo.

On my last night in the hole, I woke up to noises in the hallway. Buzzing locks. Doors slamming shut. Heavy boots moving down the empty basement corridor. Two guards, maybe three.

The footsteps grew louder and louder until they stopped outside my cell. I crawled into the corner and grabbed my sharpened toothbrush from its spot behind the sink.

The lock turned. The door swung open. I was tired and the light was dim but the second that he spoke I knew that it was Father.

He sat down on the floor beside me. He reached into his coat and offered me some chocolate. He made small talk for a while, standard bullshit questions that I answered correspondingly. Then he cleared his throat and broached the reason for his visit.

"Have you thought about what might happen, when they put you back upstairs, with the others?"

"Little bit. Be nice to have a mattress again. And I miss taking dumps with an audience."

"You know very well what I am talking about," he muttered, shaking his head.

"What about him?"

"Some people, they are not happy with how you handled things. With the way that things went down."

"He went down. That's how things went down."

"Well, yes, of course that may be true. But, nonetheless, I have heard that not everyone will celebrate your return. Just the opposite, in fact. The news is not surprising, no?"

"No, I guess not."

"The next time you are outside in the yard, you must be prepared. Things will happen quickly. There will be five or six of them. They will swarm around so that the camera view is blocked. One of them will have a shank. Plastic bottles, broken into strips, layered thick and tied together and sharpened on the concrete. If you stay near the door, the guards may break things up more quickly. But of course, this may not happen. Probably some officers will be involved."

"Do you need me for any of this? I was planning on spending my whole night staring at the wall. No offence but you're ruining the vibe."

"A dead man who tells jokes is still a dead man, no?"

"Just get to it."

"I can arrange a solution for you. I have done so for others in the past. I can do it now as well."

"For a price?"

"Oui, for a price. A process must be followed."

Father stood and lit a cigarette. The smoke curled up and hung like fog below the ceiling. Nothing moved down there without permission, not even the air.

He took another drag and blew the smoke over his shoulder then flicked the ash onto the floor and looked at me and shrugged. "Well? What do you think?"

"One question."

"Go ahead, my son."

"Who's going to protect me from you?"

EIGHT

I do my best work at the end of the month. When I'm debating which bills to ignore. When I'm saving up my pocket change for lottery tickets. When I feel like that loser kid in grade school, the one who smelled like poo and soup, the one whose mother cut his hair with scissors and a bowl. Or those kids back in high school, working part-time jobs while we tore around all night in borrowed family cars. We used to order from the drive-thru just to laugh at them. We used to toss our garbage out the window.

I do my best work when I think about these things. When I've run out of choices. When I'm desperate and ashamed.

I SHOW up midway through the meeting. Core brand purpose. Corporate social responsibility. Motivational jargon re-plagiarized from stationary bicycle celebrities and push-up challenge micro-influencers.

We finish with a photo for the company platform. Everybody leaping off the ground at once, arms thrown skyward, midriffs bared. Kiss face. Duck face. Secret agent finger pistols.

After much debate they settle on photo number seven. Then they crowd around the laptop, editing by committee. Tint, crop, filter, correct, make the fat ones skinny. Add the hashtag. Craft the tagline. Say nothing. Offend no one.

Later on they mingle near the mechanical bull, discussing themselves. Sipping cucumber infused water from old glass jars. Holding up their smartphones comparing trophy shots from recent tropical vacations. Here's me, wearing my hat in the rainforest. Here's me, sticking out my tongue while feeding french fries to a monkey. Here's me, kneeling on the beach in my cutest string bikini during the most amazing sunset.

Who are these people. Embodied avatars of their digital selves. Would they vanish in a blackout? Do they glow in the dark? They don't even notice me watching them.

THE RENTAL GROUP stumbles in at nine, still dressed in office attire. Parker hands out cheap foam cowboy hats and helps them pose for photos with the wild west props in the foyer. Fibreglass wagon wheel. Particleboard butter churn. Life sized rubber donkey.

The men head straight to the saloon. Bryce provides the wheat and barley provenance. Outlines our carbon offset strategy. Details the innovative tech solutions that drive our small batch brewing process.

The women occupy the vintage arcade in a drunken shrieking flock. Gulping white wine spritzers and sugar-free vodka seltzers, commandeering massive trays of shots. Tiny basketballs soar through tiny hoops. Cartoon go-carts race round flashing rainbow speedways. Spring loaded gophers get bashed to death by huge foam mallets.

Forty minutes left until the tournament. Parker corrals the servers in the staffroom and delegates the prep. Harper re-paints bullseyes. Piper inspects blades and handles. Zoey hands out waivers in case someone slices off a limb.

Caleb grabs the microphone and hoists himself onto the bar. Huge white teeth, big pink gums. Tight blonde curls like a wooly yellow sweater. "Welcome to Chophouse Torontooooo!"

The crowd gathers underneath him, hoisting drinks and whistling with their fingers. The music starts. Parker and Harper climb up too, clapping their hands and swaying their hips. Caleb moves to centre stage, leading the crowd through the karaoke-line-dance-sing-a-long that precedes every corporate event. Shuffling his Australian slip-on boots across the bar, snapping his suspenders and twisting his moustache, leaping up and down as the Americana-Country-Pop-Rock rhythm surges to its peak.

Bryce spots me exiting the washroom. He shuts off the blender and calls me over to the bar. Black and white striped sweater. High-waisted pleated pantaloons. Pointy black boots with shiny silver buckles.

"Were you cleaning up in there, just now?"

"I was taking a shit."

"Better grab your mop and get that done before things get crazy. Cool?"

I nod and say nothing.

"Also the recycling bins are full again. You should probably look after that. And there's a bunch of cardboard laying around back there. May as well break it all down and toss it in the dumpster while you're at it."

"Anything else?"

"Actually yeah," he says, slicing a persimmon. "Wolk is looking for you."

CHAPTER
NINE

Once a month some guy drives down from Sudbury and dumps a pile of firewood on the loading dock. They bring me in a couple nights a week to chop it up for cash.

I cut the hardwood into stove lengths and split the softwood into kindling. Then I bag it and tag it and re-stock the display case in the gift shop.

I take my third break at eleven. I walk into the staffroom and hit the lights and find Wolk, crosslegged on the tabletop, playing the banjo. He doesn't notice me at first. I back away slowly, retreating on my tiptoes like a cartoon burglar. Then my boot squeaks on a wet tile and he turns around and waves and then I'm fucked.

Tom Wolk. Assistant Manager at Chophouse Entertainment. Blue denim jacket. Checkered flannel shirt. Squeaky voice concealed by his deep public radio falsetto.

He hops down off the table and waves me to his office. Once we're both inside he locks the door and closes all the blinds. He directs me to an empty chair and plunks himself behind the desk. "Late again tonight, eh?"

"Sorry about that sir. Buses were fucked up again. Took a while getting over here."

He's instantly satisfied. "I think I'll have myself a beer. How bout it, bud?"

"Thought drinking on shift was against the rules?"

He grins and winks and shrugs. Now he's just one of the guys. We knock our cans together in an awkward toast. He leans back in his chair and discharges a loud sigh as if he's just unzipped his pants.

"Call me Tom, eh? Mister Wolk's my dad's name." He takes another sip, holding my gaze as he swallows. "Mmm. Yum. This one's triple malted. A little hoppy, but boy it sure is tasty."

The final round begins outside. Caleb's eager play-by-play booms from the speakers, rattling the windows and the thin glass panel in the door.

Wolk rotates his can in the wet ring on the desktop, edging closer to what he really wants to say.

"So you're probably sittin there wondering why we're hangin out in here, hey? Well, first of all, I gotta tell ya buddy, hell of a nice job with the firewood. Branded wood sales are way up this quarter. Way up. Great job. Just great. I really mean it."

"Thanks. It's decent money and I enjoy working alone."

"And you know, you've just got this, this kinda big burly look, and well, me and the other managers, we all had a chat, and, well, we just think you'd be a great fit for the front of house team. I mean, you see how much fun they have out there, eh? It's unmistakable!"

I stare back at him and say nothing.

"I hear you bud. Too soon. My bad. I get it. No rush, no rush at all. You just let me know, okay?"

I set the unopened can on the edge of the desk. He

reaches out and grabs my arm. The soft pads of his fingers linger gently on my skin.

"I need to get back to work."

He pulls his hand away and clears his throat. "Right. Hey, I've just gotta ask, have you thought any more about that thing we talked about a while ago?"

"I haven't thought about it at all."

"Cause, gosh, it's just that, well, as you know, I'm involved in this group, an organization really, and, well, simply put, we are one-hundred percent committed to fighting for change, but we also realize that our credibility depends on the breadth of our coalition. We need to build a big tent, right? And so we're looking for people like you, people from different backgrounds, people who can bring along diverse stories and unique experiences, people who look more like the community, y'know what I mean?"

"Remind me again what the group actually does?"

Wolk stiffens. Blood pumping, eyes alight. East coast accent becoming more and more pronounced as he paces back and forth behind the desk, pontificating like some dandruff speckled professor in a dusty campus lecture hall.

"Stories are so important in today's world, y'know? Like when it comes to inspiring important conversations in the culture. Words make stories. Stories become narratives. Narratives shape reality, right? So organizations like ours create a safe space within the culture for stories like yours..."

I watch him make his pitch. Watch his eyes moisten. Watch his skin flush pink with zeal. Who persuaded him the cause was righteous. Who convinced him it was real?

"...aren't you tired of feeling oppressed by the tyranny of problematic words? Isn't it time for an equitable lexicon? Don't you want to see yourself reflected in a more inclusive shared vocabulary? Stories are powerful and what the world needs most right now is a full-out language reboot, because inclusive narratives are the only antidote to cynicism. And that's what our group is really all about. But we need help with that, so hop on board bud! Cause, hey, if we don't get together and join the fight against cynicism, who else is gonna? Cause, gosh, an enemy is just someone whose story you haven't heard..."

He stops to catch his breath. I linger near the door, expecting an addendum to the manifesto, a moistly spoken epilogue. But Wolk says nothing further. He just looks at me, awaiting validation. He waits for me to praise his liberal values, his naked vulnerability. He waits for me to tell him that he's brave.

But when I look into his wet brown eyes, I see none of those things. I see a talented mimic. I see a dog. I see a sycophantic bootlicker bewitched by a seductive new religion.

"I'll take another look at the website."

"Okay great! It really is a neat little group. We meet up once a month. A bunch of us usually go out for drinks after. Last month we all came here and had a blast."

Imagine those meetings. Some stuffy rented room, thick with guilt. Empathy junkies. Corporate buddhists. Loud white women. Having conversations. Protecting reputations.

"Hey bud," he says, sitting down again. "Can I ask ya one more thing before ya go?"

"Go for it."

"How do ya, you know," he uses his hand to demonstrate, "chop the logs? Like in one clean chop like that? It's really neat."

I think it over for a second.

Then I tell him.

"When you split wood, it's more about the weight of the axe than the sharpness of the blade. It's not about the arms. It's in the shoulders and the torso. You gotta swing with your whole body. You gotta fully commit. You gotta follow through, in one clean motion, right down to the block. It helps if you imagine that the log is something else. Something a little less dense."

Wolk leans his elbows on the desk, chin resting in his hands, gazing back at me, fascinated.

"Normally, I imagine someone's head."

CHAPTER
TEN

Arooftop billboard says Buy One, Get One Free. The pizzas warm my fingers as I'm walking home from work. Empty white road bleeding west into the suburbs. Traffic signals swaying in the wind. The shelters are on lockdown and the bars have all gone dark. The wind whistles in the gaps between the buildings, telling secrets from a latent underworld, known to everyone yet impossible to touch.

I turn right and head north up Roncesvalles. Streetcars snowed under in the transit yard. Drunken tenant clamour emanating from the cheap motel. Handmade signs taped to lampposts and mailboxes. Abolish NATO. Fuck the WTO. People who can't afford a desktop printer, suddenly, vaguely, furious.

Only two more blocks to go. So cold I feel like running to the door. I brace the boxes on my chest and search my parka for my keys. Straggle past the coffee house and the hipster pizzeria, the dry cleaners, the cheesemonger, the place that sells expensive juice.

I spot a black sedan parked adjacent to my building.

Headlights off. Engine running. Shadowy passengers fogging up the tinted glass.

I double back and take the alleyway instead. Climb the fire escape. Squeeze in through the kitchen window. Hang my parka on the doorknob. Put the pizzas in the oven. Scrape the frost off the bedroom window, scanning up and down the block, watching for the people watching me, or the people watching them. But nothing's out there. The black sedan is gone. The street belongs to winter.

I turn on the radio. Traffic every ten minutes. Sports after business and weather. Extreme cold warning in effect, exposed skin will freeze in under three minutes. Trains and flights cancelled. Schools and highways closed. Homeless man found dead on busy downtown sidewalk. Are you ready for this weekend's blizzard? Stay safe and up to date with our special coverage. Weather brought to you by Binoxin. Free yourself from nail fungus. Ask your doctor about Binoxin Gel.

Back outside I breathe into my fists and flick the lighter till it sparks. I lean against the cold brick wall, smoking, watching smoke curl from the chimneys of the old narrow houses to the east. Plow trucks rumbling in the distance. Loose snow twisting thinly in the street. Destitute trees, isolated on the boulevards, bare branches rattling like bones in the wind.

The shop door opens underneath me. Dreamy pop songs drift up the fire escape like invitations. Between the tracks I hear the click and clatter of her hand tools, the dull repeated thud of her heavy cooler doors. I want to wander down and ask her how she's doing. Suggest we meet up sometime for a drink. Tell her I've been thinking about her. Tell her my real name.

Everything sounds great inside my head. But under these conditions, how would I even start? New clothing, a shave and a haircut, furniture, socks, dishes, sheets. Money. I would need some money.

"READ A LOT OF THAT STUFF?"

"What stuff?"

"Dystopian fiction."

"Guess so. Seems like the only option lately. How bout you?"

"Used to."

"How come you stopped?"

"It all came true."

She wrinkled her nose and put her hands on her hips. "Come up with that in advance?"

"Maybe."

"Clever."

I said goodbye and wandered to a different section. It was a Sunday in November and the little store was busy despite the early winter chill. I was bored and lonely and broke and used books were the only entertainment I could afford.

I was in the check-out line when she tapped me on the shoulder.

"Hey dude. Me again. You live around here?"

"Moved in down the street around six weeks ago. How come?"

"Nothing much. Just doing a little research. Local demographics, foot traffic, anecdotal data from random dudes like you. You know, all that nerdy retail stuff."

I couldn't help but laugh. "Why on earth are you doing that?"

She grinned. "Cause I'm an entrepreneur, you dick."

"For real?"

"Fuck yeah for real. I'm a big time florist. Opening up my own shop in like a month."

"That's exciting. Good for you."

"Aw shucks. Dude stop making me blush."

"Next time I'm heading to a funeral, maybe I'll stop by."

"For sure. Funerals, weddings, birthdays, New Years, Valentine's, Saint Paddy's—"

"Saint Patrick's Day?" I interrupted. "You're a big shamrock producer or something?"

"The very biggest."

"Well I'm dropping by for sure then. Not till March though, obviously."

"Obviously."

A few weeks later a power saw woke me up around six. Sunday was my only morning off and getting up early was the last thing I felt like doing. But sleep was off the table, so I got cleaned up and went downstairs to check things out.

The scene inside the shop that morning was like one of those home renovation shows on television. Contractors tearing out the ceiling. Movers hauling boxes from a truck. Refrigeration guys and telecom guys and a couple guys on ladders putting a new electric sign above the door. In the middle of the chaos, wearing rubber clogs and overalls and drinking coffee from a thermos, was the green-eyed girl from the bookstore.

"Congratulations," I said, walking up from behind. "I would have brought flowers, but..."

It took her a second to recognize my face. "Upstairs? You?"

I nodded.

"That's crazy!"

"Hey, since I'm awake early and everything," I said, rolling my eyes. "Need any help down here?"

"Absolutely dude. Look at all this shit."

I followed her outside. We both grabbed boxes from the truck. On the way back in, I asked her for her name.

"Zahra," she said, blushing. "My name is Zahra."

HEAT BILLOWS from the kitchen window, coaxing me indoors. I shuffle forward and lean against the rail. I focus on smoking. I watch the storm clouds thicken like a shroud above the lake. I do this for a long time. Until I'm numb. Until my bad ideas freeze to death.

The oven timer beeps. I climb inside and scoop the pizzas from the rack. Plop down on the recliner, eating off my lap. Smoking joints and watching highlights of the game.

I smoke a little more and imagine that I'm there, inside the arena. Knees jammed up against the seats. Boot soles sticking to the floor. Smell of draft beer and pretzels and hot dogs. The crowd rising to its feet as the puck trickles slowly through the crease.

But I won't be there again. No more dinners in a private box. No more thirty dollar drinks inside the lounge. You'll never catch a glimpse of me on television, eating poutine in the platinum level seats, grinning smugly with my arm around a blonde. Hockey is a telecom duopoly. Highlights are as close as I can get.

I skip the post-game show and watch a black and white film instead. There's a private dick with a doting secretary and his fee is fifty bucks a day. There's a crooked cop and a femme fatale and a double-cross you know is coming. It's always night and it's always raining and the detective always drinks alone. I mute the volume and say their lines out loud, making up the story as I go.

A noise downstairs wakes me up around three. Change of pressure in the stairwell. Nimble footsteps climbing softly up the steps.

I reach beneath the chair and slide the hatchet from its holster. The floorboards creak behind the door. The mail slot hinges open. Something made of paper hits the floor. For a moment nothing happens. And then the same deliberate footsteps descend slowly to the street.

The wind dies in the vestibule as the lower door slams shut. I drop the hatchet and close my eyes. I don't need to open the envelope. I already know what's inside.

THURSDAY

CHAPTER
ELEVEN

L ately I've been having this recurring dream. It's summertime and I'm a little kid. Younger brother snoring on the bottom bunk beneath me. Parents both asleep in the room across the hall. The lamp on the dresser is dimmed down low and the red cotton shade throws an eery ruby pattern on the wall.

Mother never shut the drapes. Outside, the darkness is absolute. Like swimming out into deep water and looking down. If there's nothing lurking in those ancient fathoms, why is the lake there at all?

It's been a long hot summer and hot all week and the air inside the cabin is thick and damp and still. I unzip my sleeping bag and stretch out on top. The nylon shell feels cool against my skin. I roll onto my side and close my eyes. And then I hear the footsteps.

That squeaky floorboard in the kitchen. Log walls groaning in the hall. Long heavy strides. Hard shoes with heels. It's not that the intruder is clumsy or inept, it's worse than that. This intruder wants to be heard.

The footsteps stop behind my bedroom door. I push my

face into the pillow and count to ten. Maybe it will go away. Maybe it did already.

I peer down over the edge of the bunk. There's nothing in the doorway. Then the hinges creak. And the door swings open by itself.

I cower back against the wall and cover my face with my arms. Why aren't my parents waking up? Why isn't my little brother screaming?

I hold my breath and look between my fingers. In the doorway there's a towering stranger, stooping just to fit inside the room. Long black robe. Black hat bent against the ceiling. Smell of burnt hair and shit.

It brushes past the bed and stands before the window, uttering incantations in a strange unholy language, summoning its minions from the forest's darkest depths.

And then it stiffens.

As though it feels my gaze.

I shut my eyes and this time I'm praying. I don't know how to pray or who I'm praying to but I'm praying as hard as I can.

The monster turns and steps toward the bed. My heart sinks. I say a final prayer and look up at the face. Pale green skin. Long crooked nose. Blank black eyes, rimmed in fire.

The witch grins and opens her mouth. Rank breath wafting from her cavernous throat. Thick tongue quivering like a slug. Her mouth opens wider and wider, filling up the room, deforming her skull. I hear her jawbone snap. I watch her skin stretch until it rips. Then she licks her greasy lips and swallows me whole.

CHAPTER
TWELVE

The diner is a tavern after dark. Bar down one side. Booths down the other. Washrooms in the basement. The bartender nods toward the empty seats. "Sit wherever you want."

I buy a drink at the bar and choose a booth near the back. Lazy jazz hums from unseen speakers. The neon sign above the window floods the road in emerald green. The other buildings on the street are empty and quiet and dark, like facades in the background of a painting.

The note said Thursday night at nine. I'm late, but not late enough to matter. I take a drink. The beer tastes awful. Like hand soap or detergent. I choke it down and focus on the room.

Three patrons perched on barstools, a woman and two men. The woman wears a red sleeveless dress and has her back turned to the street. Young and slender and bored. Leaning on her elbow and studying her fingernails. The man to her right is somewhat older, with a narrow face and a long hawkish nose. He looks impatient. They're both drinking coffee and seem to know each other. The second man sits alone, on the long side of the bar, facing the coffee cisterns and the mirrored wall of booze. He's drinking whiskey from a tumbler and his pale grey hat is the same colour as his skin.

A black sedan stops outside the diner. The chauffeur hops out quickly, straightening his uniform, combing his beard with his fingers. He shuffles his feet and takes two deep breaths and gently knocks on the window.

The rear door swings open. A man passes from the back-seat to the street, hidden briefly by exhaust smoke swirling low along the road. He steps through the haze and onto the sidewalk, a perfect black silhouette set against the billowing white backdrop. Then he enters the diner. Hooded black overcoat. Leather boots and gloves. Face obscured in shadow.

My eyes are getting heavy. My face is melting off my skull. The lighting flickers. A tremor rocks the building and the room lurches to the right. The walls ooze thin red grease. Orange sludge engulfs the floor. Fissures spread like veins across the ceiling seeping glowing bright green slime. A whirlpool churns backwards in the centre of the room, swallowing context, drowning nuance, revealing a counterfeit world.

I glance toward the bar, expecting panic. Shrieks of terror. Trembling tint-stained hands. But the others haven't moved. They just sit there, bleeding colour. Pigment pours down their bodies, dripping from their arms and ankles, collecting in rank beige puddles on the floor. The diner fades to muddy sepia. Binary. Monochrome. This is the world.

The woman in red stirs her coffee. The hawk nosed man adjusts his tie. The other man swirls his glass and takes a drink. And then I understand. These people are imposters.

Stock characters in a movie or a video game. If I sit here long enough, the loop will finish and start over again.

The hooded man strides past the bar. Footsteps splashing on the wet tile floor, face still veiled in shadow. And I can't help but stare. Transfixed by this reality. Bewildered by our black and white world.

He stops at my booth and takes off his coat. Black wool turtleneck, tight black slacks. Slender through the shoulders with firm upturned breasts. Why did I assume it was a man. Why not a woman. Why not some other creature?

She slides into the seat across from me.

"You're a difficult man to find."

"Doesn't seem like you had much trouble."

"I suppose you're right."

She lays a folder on the table and pushes it across. Strange dark eyes. Dusty golden skin. High wide cheeks with a small smug mouth.

"Let me save you some time," I tell her. "I'm retired. I don't do this anymore."

"Forgive me," she says dryly. "But I beg to differ."

I stare back at her.

"Confused? Of course you are. Allow me a moment to explain. You see, I've recently purchased your debt. Well, that's not entirely true either. My firm, rather, has purchased your debt. And while one could deem this sort of acquisition risky or unconventional, the fact is, at the moment, we find ourselves in dire need of your services. How does this affect you? It's really quite simple. Once the value of services rendered equals the total amount owing, you shall be released from said contract..."

She goes on with her proposal but the words stop making sense. Noise slips through her lips like music, low and languid and smooth. Sophisticated vocabulary, subtle mix of different foreign accents, speaking in absolute terms, as if I've already agreed, as if my presence alone constitutes my consent. Then she opens the folder and explains the job. And I know for certain this is Father's doing.

CHAPTER
THIRTEEN

The kid stares up from the photograph. Mid-twenties. Blonde hair. Dimples. Clear white skin and straight white teeth. Blurry summertime objects in the background, wildflowers, tree trunks, young people lounging on patterned blankets in the grass. I pinch my leg beneath the table to keep myself awake.

"Who's this?"

"He's called Colin Fowst. Current whereabouts unknown. We had another chap tailing him, but now he's vanished as well."

"Sounds like a trap."

"Indeed."

"Who's looking for him?"

"My firm, of course."

"Who's really looking for him?"

"Good lord," she rolls her eyes. "That's really none of your business, is it?"

"Let me guess. He owes you money?"

"Our firm has been retained to settle his account. My partners and I felt that hiring someone like you might expedite the process."

"What have you got so far?"

"Precious little, I'm afraid. Public records and social media yielded nothing consequential. His financials led us to an unoccupied apartment in Etobicoke. Of course, he left no forwarding address. But our man found some mail in the lobby. It's all there inside the folder."

The envelopes are mostly junk but there's one marked confidential.

"Shall I?"

She nods. "I insist."

I tear it open. It's a 2017 Income Tax statement.

"It's his T4."

"I figured that," she says, sounding bored. "So you've got you first lead. Where, may I ask, was young Fowst last employed?"

"Seventy-seven Roncesvalles."

"Down the street from your little flat? Interesting."

I'm not sure what she means by that, so I let it slide. "Why you wouldn't just call the cops? Hire a skip trace or a real detective?"

"As I'm sure you've gathered by now, this is a delicate matter. Our clients require a degree of discretion. Their privacy must be guaranteed." She checks her watch. "Have you any further questions? It really is quite late."

"Just a few more. Let's say I find this kid. Fowst? That his name? So I go out and find little Fowst. Then what?"

She opens a thin gold case and hands me a stiff black business card. "Call this number. My firm takes care of the rest."

"That's it?"

"Indeed. In fact, should you find him by midnight on Sunday, you'll be paid a small bonus."

"Why Sunday?"

"Frankly, I have no idea. My clients hire people like me

so they don't have to answer questions like that, particularly from people like you."

"Last question."

"I'm on the edge of my seat."

"What if I say no?"

"I beg your pardon?"

"You heard me. I tell you no thanks then stand up and walk out the door. What happens then?"

"Finish your drink."

"What?"

"I said finish you drink."

Her tone compels obedience. I lift the glass and swallow what's left. She pulls an object from her coat and flicks her wrist. The envelope rotates once in the air and hits the table with a heavy monied thud. Melted wax seal. Lavish black paper. My new name stamped across the front in gold.

"Go ahead," she says. "Open it."

I hesitate.

She blinks and gazes back at me. A toxic, commodifying gaze. A gaze that tells me I'm an object and this meeting is a transaction. And yet despite her cold appraisal I remain enchanted. Enraptured and repelled. Unable to flee or acquiesce.

I take a long deep breath and brace myself against the table. Her lips curl into a lecherous grin and she begins to laugh. And then a thrill ripples through me and I fall into her gaping mouth. Floating there, alone in the void, I see visions of my future self. There's a winter storm and a huge empty house and I'm locked inside a small cold room, shackled on my knees before a monster. Flames surround me. Fresh blood coats the floors. I'm bleeding from the torso and my face is cut to ribbons.

The vision collapses, exploding like confetti. The music stops. The hawk nosed man stands up. The woman in red rises next to him. The second man turns and slides his hand inside his coat. Three sets of eyes. Six lifeless blanks. Drones. Summoned here to tear me apart.

She speaks to me again. Moist lips birthing soft whispers that crawl across my skin like insects, occupying crevices, penetrating every orifice. She's inside me now. Wearing my skin like a mask. I try and get away but I can barely lift my arms. Nearly blind, cold dead muscles turned to rust. I feel her sensing my exhaustion. Feel her savour my paralysis. The drones rise and begin to chant. My lips move, but it's her words that exit my mouth.

"I'll do it."

We say this together.

And in the moments that follow her face is like nothing I've seen before or even recognize. Her dark brown eyes have turned to fire. Her smile wraps right around her skull, as if her face may tilt back and break behind the bloody stump of her jaw.

THE KITCHEN DOOR SWINGS OPEN. The bartender walks out and ties his apron. He takes the towel off his shoulder, whistling a tune, polishing glassware, wiping down the bar. The radio is on again. The drones are at their seats. The woman in my booth hasn't spoken for a while and I start to wonder if tonight is even real, if I'm dead or dreaming or something worse.

"So how do I contact you?"

"Quite simply," she says, buttoning her coat. "You do not."

"Tell me your name at least."

She pulls her hood over her head. "Call me Hera."

"That your real name?"

"People like us don't have real names. You know this."

She turns around and walks briskly out the door. The black sedan rolls away, exhaust fumes fading from white to grey and then dissolving into nothing.

What make was the car. How tall was the driver. What the fuck just happened?

But it's too late for asking questions. There's no space left in my head for anything but money. Say goodbye to nightshifts at the Chophouse. Say farewell to fucking John and Kev.

At the time it felt like a mistake. It still feels like one right now. But once the money hit the table, what other choice did I have?

There's no such thing as choices. This world runs on scarcity. This world runs on need and inertia.

CHAPTER
FOURTEEN

B ack outside it's still too cold to breathe. The kind of weather that reminds me of my childhood. Burst pipes. Frozen locks. Real winters, when there were four seasons instead of two.

The neon sign shuts off above me. The bartender moves around the empty diner, clearing tables and switching off the lights. The last lamp dies and the glass goes dark and the windowpane becomes a mirror. My reflection stares out from his obsolete universe, dingy and distorted yet somehow strangely real. He lights a joint and strolls away backwards, smoking, watching the hot neon letters turn black in the cold.

I head west along Queen Street. Back alleys crawling with addicts. Far right cops cruising for easy busts and risky sex. Sickly figures haunting rooming house windows, gazing out at other strangers, left palms pressed against the glass for balance, right fists pumping sadly into cumstained thrift store drapes.

I turn around and take the long way home instead. Straight up Lansdowne, past the public school and the community centre. Past tall narrow houses with fenced-in lawns and porches. Past the fire hall and the grocery store. Beneath the overpass and up the hill and left toward the bridge. The sky is clear and the stars are bright and the moon is a cold white sun, emitting dimness and silence and nothing else at all.

Headlights coming fast over the bridge. The car slows and I lock eyes with the driver as she passes. Straight blonde hair, freckles on her cheeks and nose. She looks familiar and I wonder where she's going and what she's doing out so late.

Once the car is out of sight it's clear that I had no idea who she was, that she just looked like someone I know, or someone that I've known in the past, or someone that I've seen in the movies or on television. People look so similar. On certain days I feel like every person on the street might be somebody I know.

I stop to light a joint. Looking south the bridge feels like a cliff. The railway tracks curve east and disappear, an iron road travelled only by machines and those machines have left behind.

Beyond the rails the lake is like a confrontation. Black waves roil and heave against the shore, tearing off huge white slabs that bob and drift in the nearby slush like freshly severed limbs.

I drop the roach and step on it. On the ground beside my foot there's a set of paw tracks in the snow. The trail stretches back along the bridge as if the creature had been following me home. Raccoon tracks. Like the dead one in the gutter yesterday.

Weird noises in the dark behind me. Dry twigs snapping. Dead leaves blowing in the wind. I light another joint and start walking. I hear the noise again and turn around and see the dead raccoon trundling behind me like a dog. We walk along together until the bridge meets the road. The raccoon stops and taps my leg. In the shadows, up ahead, I catch sight of something strange. There's a man standing in the middle of the street, blocking my path.

Do I approach him?

Do I run?

He lurches forward before I can decide. Injured or disabled, odd shadow staggering a few steps behind, both of them limping toward me like weirdly conjoined twins. He passes underneath a lamppost. Thick through his chest and shoulders. Long black parka. Black toque and blue jeans and boots with bright red laces. He's got my body and my clothes. Perhaps he's got my face as well.

He carries all his weight on his one good leg. A hard stomp that echoes down the block. Breath puffing out in hot white spurts. Plastic bag banging off his shin. Steady pounding rhythm keeping time like a clock, like a godforsaken pendulum. We're only steps apart when at last I see his face. Cooked red skin. Angry scar across his cheek. Upper lip twisted and diseased. Except his eyes are truly beautiful, the purest brightest blue. In total contradiction with the rest of him. Does he shop at night to avoid the stares. Does he have any family or friends. Does he work. Does he fuck?

I imagine life inside his small apartment. Avoiding the world beyond his walls. Tending to houseplants and a series of pets. Adulthood measured out in medical appointments and fast food deliveries and superhero movie sequels.

I see him as an old man. Tired of television shows and bingo in the common room and sitting in his own shit. Tired of everything but not quite out of time. Still convinced that things could change.

I see him on a gurney with a tube stuck up his nose. He's realized his whole life was spent hoping for things that were never going to happen. He knows he's going to die alone. He wonders who will attend his funeral, or if there will even be one.

I think about all that and I'm washed in shame. I take a step closer. I want to look at him without flinching. I want to tell him that he'll be okay. That the city is full of lonely people. People sitting by themselves on park benches. People riding buses, eyes glazed, wearing earbuds and staring at the floor. People all alone at the movies, laughing when everyone else laughs.

I'm about to speak when he starts to cough. Clutching his chest, spitting up bile and little chunks of puke. Drool swings from his chin and the snotty film around his lips sprays a sick wet mist with every desperate gasping breath.

He falls and grabs my coat for balance. Church bells echo through the streets. I lift my arm and smash it down into his face. I hit him as hard as I can, again and again, until he crumples at my feet. Prone and shuddering on the icy west-end pavement. Glossy ropes of blood strewn across his boiled beaten face. I bend over him and listen. Somehow, he's still breathing. I flick my lighter and move the flame toward his face and the eyes staring back are my own.

FRIDAY

FIFTEEN

I t was raining when I woke up and it's raining even harder now. Inbound traffic's at a standstill. The streets are swamped in slush. The sky is a dead grey dome.

The queue at the cafe stretches halfway round the block. I cut the line and slip inside. Local artwork, mismatched chairs, assorted cacti and taxidermy. People complain about being too busy but they'll wait around forever for a special drink.

A barista takes orders looking bored and aloof. Her name tag says her name is Chelsea. Round wire framed glasses. Closely cropped brown hair. Faded green top tucked into high-waisted stone washed jeans. The kind of person you might see working in a record store or a comic book shop, not some bullshit place like this.

There's a skinny guy preparing food behind the counter. Orange beanie. Pony tail. Blending ten dollar smoothies, spreading nut butter on gluten-free scones, smiling oddly as he moves his aproned body to the corporate playlist, another flaccid stream of pop songs written by committees of machines.

Chelsea gives no shits. The line moves slowly. I linger near the till, hoping someone will acknowledge my presence. I watch the local news on television. Stock quotes for people with no money. Traffic reports for people who don't drive. A failed actor turned failed journalist assuring us that somewhere, news has happened.

Chelsea finally glances my way. "Happy Friday. Can I get you something?"

"I need to speak to the manager."

She looks me up and down and rolls her eyes. "Our manager's actually in a meeting right now," she says in a drowsy voice, like she's exhausted by the act of speaking. "Is there something I could help you with instead?"

I pull out Hera's business card.

Chelsea's eyes widen.

"No," I tell her. "There isn't."

CHAPTER
SIXTEEN

"Come on in!"

A young woman holding a phone on a stick greets me at the office door. Sleeveless collared blouse. Pencil skirt. Thin toned arms and lean tanned legs and symmetrically perfect eyebrows. "I just love the way I look on my phone. Oh my gosh—does that sound vain? I'm sorry."

I flash Hera's card and give her my new name.

"Skylar," she says, reaching out to shake my hand. "Sorry about the wait, we're short staffed right now and it's actually been so crazy. So are you like a lawyer or something?"

"No, I've been retained to locate someone. Does the name 'Colin Fowst' ring a bell?"

"Oh my God. I hope he's not like in trouble or anything."

"Nothing like that. His family hasn't heard from him in quite some time. They're getting very worried."

"Well, for starters, he hasn't worked here for a while."

"How long?"

"Six or seven months? He left around the time I started.

Chelsea's been here the longest. She seemed to know him pretty well."

"What kind of person was he? Anything that stood out? Anything unusual or strange?"

"He was a decent guy. Good looking, about your height and weight, maybe a touch shorter. He was into sports and clothes and real estate. He talked about money a lot. Not the best employee to be honest, always showing up late, always super grumpy, always leaving early for appointments. He was actually pretty annoying to deal with. I mean, there was this one time..."

Skylar goes on a while longer. Chewing her gum. Playing with her hair. Fried frayed voice like a goat. I can't tell if she's stupid or just acting that way. Eventually I stop listening altogether. If there was something suspicious about Fowst, I doubt this woman would have noticed.

"What about his social media?"

"Yah? What about it?"

"Is he on your list?"

"My list," she chuckles. "You mean my feed? Just a sec."

She logs in to her account and suddenly her face dominates the screen, an endless grid of nearly identical self-portraits. Close-up shots of manicures and brunch. A monetized french bulldog named Chloe. The blurb beneath her profile photo includes a list of other talents. Certified Mindfulness Coach. Yoga Teacher Candidate. Recipe Designer. Curator. Activist. Human Being.

"You forgot Coffee Shop Manager."

"Yah, I won't be working here much longer though," she says, blushing. "So I'd rather be more aspirational with my social media content. You know, put your goals out into the universe and be a good kind person and eventually the universe will make it happen, that whole thing."

"Right. That whole thing."

We scroll through Fowst's page. It's basically trash. Sports highlights, movie trailers, grumpy cats and dancing babies. No political posts. No links to any weird accounts. No tags or family photos. Nothing personal at all.

"Sorry," she says, fake-pouting with her bottom lip. "Is there anything else I can do?"

"I think that's it for now. Hope we catch a break soon though, hate to have to turn things over to the cops."

"Hey wait," she blurts, sounding frantic. "Why don't you check his locker?" She gets up and opens the door and bumps straight into Chelsea.

"Hey boss," Chelsea says, sounding meek and unconvincing. "Need your help rebooting the POS when you get a minute."

Skylar leads me further down the hallway, glancing at her reflection on every surface that we pass. Chelsea hovers just behind us, canvas sneakers scuffling in the dust. We stop at a row of lockers across from the staff washroom. There's a whiteboard on the wall with a weekly work schedule displayed in brightly coloured marker.

"It's the middle one."

"Are you going to open it, or should I?"

"Oh, they don't lock," she says. "Go ahead and search away."

I nod toward the washroom.

"I'll get started in a minute."

I SHUT the washroom door and lock it. Run both taps and press my ear against the door. Hurried footsteps moving back toward the office. Skylar's high heeled shoes clicking hard against the floor.

"Holy shit. Holy shit. Holy shit."

"Relax," Skylar says. "I handled it."

"Handled what? Who the hell is this friggin guy?"

"No idea. But we got rid of Colin's shit like months ago, remember? So it's all good. Besides, there's nothing in that locker but a random pile of crap. Nothing that can link us to what happened."

"What DID happen?"

"I don't even know. I don't want to. Neither do you."

"Friggin Colin. I knew something would go wrong. You think he's really missing?"

"You could always go see him and find out for yourself."

"True," says Chelsea. "Okay let's talk later. There's a total stranger in our bathroom right now."

"I know, right? I was actually shitting my pants at first."

"Who hired him?"

"No idea. Some weird company."

They pause for a second while one of them unwraps a mint or a candy or something.

"Hey guess who's moving up a level soon?"

Chelsea gasps. "You lie."

"I'm serious. I'm so pumped. You don't even know. What level are you at these days?"

"Meh. Still a proxy."

"That sucks. How come?"

"Lots of reasons I guess. Got sick and missed a few weeks. Then my blood test expired and it took another couple weeks to get a new one. So yeah it was this whole big thing. But I'm back on the list now, back in good standing or whatever."

"Aw that's great! Maybe I'll see you there this weekend. But listen we shouldn't be talking about this at work. You know the rules."

"Yep," Chelsea snorts. "Took me like a month to memo-rize them."

. . .

FOWST'S LOCKER is as useless as his social media. An old pair of sneakers, a mouldy white towel, an expired health club membership hanging on a red and white lanyard. It's a head shot, a better photo than the one in Hera's folder. Dull blue eyes. Thick blonde hair cut short. A rosy boyish blush on his pale white cheeks. Self-assured, but for no real reason. The way someone on a rowing team might look.

I tell Skylar thanks on my way out the door. Then I catch a glimpse of Chelsea and decide to stick around. Something contrived about her movements and mannerisms, a phoney quality that had been absent before. She looks guilty and uncomfortable. She looks like she wishes I would leave.

I line up for a coffee. Chelsea serves the other customers, gazing elsewhere, evading scrutiny. When I finally place my order she still won't look me in the eye.

"Busy day?"

"Yep," she mutters, sliding my change across the counter. "It's been murder around here lately."

On the giant screen behind us, The Politician makes his televised debut. Buffed and tanned and slicked. Stuffed into a dark blue suit. Hollow men lined up on stage behind him, crooked fingers crossed. He reads the speech with difficulty, halting proclamations confused by laboured breathing and mispronounced jargon. He's going to stop the gravy train. He's putting money in our pockets. He's a regular guy, just like us. He's for the people.

And this is how it starts. No clandestine meetings in dimly lit rooms. No shadowy men paying bribes. No secrets to uncover. No mysteries to solve. It happens in broad daylight, in plain english, with a folksy dogwhistle ruse that dupes the farm belts and the suburbs and the dying towns up north. Nostalgia for a golden age that never was. A promise of renewal so impossible to keep.

But let's see him come down here, with the servant class. Stocking shelves all night at the supermarket. Working extra jobs at Christmas just to earn enough to pay for gifts. Driving taxis, cleaning houses, delivering food on a bike in the rain. Trading time for money until there's no time left to trade.

Come down.

Tread water with us.

Come down here and drown with the people.

CHAPTER SEVENTEEN

C helsea's shift ends at two. I eat lunch at home and change into my uniform. Grab a clipboard and a pen. Head back to the cafe and hang around nearby until she leaves.

I tail her to the bottom of Roncesvalles. She lines up at the streetcar stop, wringing her hands in the rain. She waits there for a few minutes until she loses patience and sets out on foot. I stay about a block behind her, heading east along King Street, downtown skyline growing larger in the distance. The Tower coming slowly into view.

She stops outside a yellowbrick mid-rise building halfway up Jameson. I walk past until I'm out of sight then double back and watch her from across the street. Punching numbers on the buzzer system. Waiting in the vestibule for a response that never comes.

She tries the buzzer a few more times. She takes out her phone and makes a call. Her face gets cloudy. Her shoulders slump. She jams the phone into her pocket and saunters out into the rain, looking confused and tired and sad. I wait until she turns the corner. Then I head inside and get to work.

The Superintendent meets me in the lobby. Light blue shirt. Dark blue slacks. Bald on top with bushy grey eyebrows and long white sideburns. We shake hands and shoot the shit. I don't remember his name and I'm pretty sure he doesn't remember mine.

"Where's Johnny and the kid?"

"Just me today. Here for a walk-through."

He makes a face. "Don't think we have anybody in arrears."

"Head Office didn't call down about this one?"

"News to me," he chuckles. "But that doesn't always matter, does it?"

I hand him the fake paperwork and fold my arms across my chest.

"Damn eyes," he says, patting his pockets for his glasses. "Which unit did you say?"

"It's on there somewhere. Last name is Fowst."

He squints and scans the form. Halfway through page one he shrugs and hands it back. "Good enough for the girls we go with, eh partner?" He goes into the office and comes back out with a keyring bolted to a battered wooden stick. "So they float," he grins. "Case you drop em down the toilet."

"Good idea."

"6B's your guy. Turn left off the elevator, then straight down to the end of the hall." He pries off the key and drops it in my palm. "Fowst, eh? Funny. Never gave us any trouble. Before now of course."

"Trouble happens sometimes."

"Yessir it most certainly does. It is what it is, as they say. It is what it is. That there's the sixth floor master key. Need her back before you leave. I go on lunch around noon. Usually take a few hours. If no one's here when you get done, slide her underneath the door."

. . .

WALKING into Fowst's apartment is like entering another building altogether. Clean white walls. Glossy hardwood floors. Not the shithole I'd been expecting. The lights are off and the blinds are shut and the only sound is a leaky faucet dripping somewhere in the dark.

I pull my gloves on and hit the lights. The front hall closet looks more like a sporting goods store. Dirt caked mountain bike. Crates of camping gear. A rolled-up canvas tent. Dumbbells and kettle bells and a lime green rubber yoga ball. Half a dozen jackets. Pricey boots and sneakers. A fancy black tuxedo sheathed in dry cleaners plastic.

The kitchen is completely spotless. White pine cabinets above a white tile backsplash. Speckled granite countertop. Stainless steel dishwasher with matching fridge and stove. Nice place for a guy who worked in a coffee shop.

Vertical blinds cast diagonal lines across the living room floor. Glass and metal coffee table. Vintage brass bar cart. Brown leather sofa on a white shag rug. A floor lamp arches up from a heavy marble base, hovering above the furniture like an orbiting planet.

There's a big framed print hanging on the wall that doesn't fit with the decor. Two dimensional, vaguely medieval, more like an illustration than a painting. The man in the image wears a plain white tunic beneath a long purple robe and for a belt he wears a snake. He stands before a low stone altar covered in strange gold objects, surrounded by flowers and foliage. His right hand points up and his left hand points down and his eyes seem to follow me around.

Beneath the painting there's an apartment-sized tree sprouting up from a white ceramic planter. Soil sprinkled thinly near the pot's outer edge, missed by the vacuum or the broom. I bend over and grab the trunk, wiggling gently

87

back and forth until it's loose enough to be removed. I lift it out and set it down. The ball of soil around the roots stays perfectly intact. It's wrapped in cellophane.

The pot's lower section is a hidden compartment crammed to the brim with medication. Small red pills vacuum sealed in clear plastic bags. Six bags total. A couple hundred pills per bag. I don't know what they are or who they're for, but a thousand of anything is usually worth something.

I pocket two bags and leave the rest alone. I put the tree back on top and brush the dirt off the floor. The man in the painting watches me work. How many crimes has he witnessed. How many secrets has he kept safe?

The bedroom looks copied from the magazines on the coffee table. King sized bed on a low wood frame. Night stands and an armoire and a dresser. A big wooden desk that looks old but likely isn't.

On the wall above the desk there's a photo montage arranged in stylish oddly sized frames. Colin at a concert with his arm around a girl. Colin in box seats at the game. Colin leaning on a sleek blue car wearing a bright pink tank top. Pop star biceps. Dimples. A pretty-boy with aspirations.

There's some family photos too. An old black and white shot of his grandparents, back when people didn't smile for pictures. A garden portrait with his parents and a young girl, perhaps a sister or a cousin. A family reunion in a hill top park, three generations, dressed in formal clothing, back-dropped by the sea.

The desk itself is pretty standard. Three drawers down the side plus one in the middle for a keyboard. Scraps of paper tacked below the photos, bills and receipts and to-do lists, reminders jotted down on sticky notes, phone numbers scrawled on napkins.

The top two drawers are nearly full. Obsolete chargers

and dried-out highlighters. A lifetime supply of paper clips. Everyday crap that people store in desks.

The bottom drawer is bigger and it's locked. I take a steak knife from the kitchen and shove it in the slot. The little lock won't budge.

I grab the handle and set my feet and rip the drawer from the desk. It breaks apart in mid-air and spills its contents on the floor. External hard drive. Tablet computer. Thin silver laptop.

I search his clothing next. Pre-rolled joints amongst his underwear and socks. Unused condoms in a bathrobe pocket. A twenty dollar bill inside a ragged pair of jeans.

I find a black wool blazer in the armoire. I take it off the hanger and turn it upside down and something heavy falls out and bounces on the carpet. It's a cheap pay-as-you-go flip phone. A burner phone, like mine.

The decorator never bothered with the bathroom. Pale yellow shower curtain. Lime green tile. Like a shitty motel in Central Florida. Real estate brochures piled on the counter. Lifestyle mags in a rack beside the toilet, sports car road tests, wristwatch buyers guides, how to give your wife an orgasm. There's blood spattered in the sink and bloody smears on all the cabinets and blood soaked rags stuffed into the trash. Someone started cleaning up, but stopped early. Or got stopped.

I open up the medicine cabinet. Body spray in a stout black can. Shaving cream and dental floss and a black plastic comb. Orange bottle of expired antibiotics, bloody finger-prints smudged across the label.

I glance at my reflection in the mirror. Behind me, there's a shape behind the shower curtain. A shadow. Like someone crouching in the tub.

I turn around and sneak toward the bathtub. I take a long deep breath. Then I rip the curtain sideways.

It's a black dress shirt discarded in a rumpled pile on the top edge of the tub. I hook it with my finger and lift it up into the light. Thick French collar. Wide French cuffs. Pearly stains spewed across the chest like glue. Ejaculate. Too much to be from just one person. Good thing I'm wearing gloves. In the bottom of the tub there's a long steel chain. One end's been severed with a hacksaw. The other end is welded to a heavy iron collar.

I leave the room exactly how I found it. I'm getting low on time. So far this is interesting stuff, but there's nothing here that proves he's even missing, let alone something worse. The smartest move might be to hang around and wait. See if he comes back. See who comes back with him. And yeah, the cops may want to take a look. I'll call them when I find a body. From a payphone.

The last stop is the walk-in closet. The door's shut tight. I turn the knob and nudge it open. Besides a few bare hangers, it looks completely empty. I flip on the lights to make sure. The carpet's been removed and there's a symbol painted on the floor:

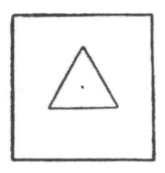

Thick white candles melted down to stumps form a circle around the square. I lift my phone to snap a photo, but something on the wall catches my eye. A couple inches off the floor, brushed on by hand in the same gold paint, there's a message: HE WHO SEEKS THE GODDESS SEEKS THE END.

I read it out loud like a spell. And then somebody knocks on the apartment door. I sprint back over to the desk. Slide the laptop down my pants and cinch my belt to hold it steady. Pocket the phone and the hard drive and the tablet. Snatch the notes and scraps of paper off the wall.

There's a second knock, louder this time.

I kill the lights and pull my gloves off as I'm jogging to the door. I hold my breath and press my eye against the peephole. The hall seems way too dark, like someone busted out the lights. A blurry shoulder drifts into view, lingers for a moment, then drifts back out again. I make a fist and open the door.

It's a short skinny kid with icy blue eyes and a squashed up face like a rat. Puffy red coat three sizes too big. Unlaced leather boots. Black and gold flat brimmed cap pulled down over his eyes. He lifts his chin and cocks his head to the side.

"Yo. Fowst home?"

"Haven't seen him."

His eyes narrow. "Know where he went?"

"We're inspecting the smoke detectors today. Most tenants don't come back until we're done."

"Okay," he says, nodding. "Okay. I'll hit him up later."

I step into the hallway and lock the door behind me. When I turn around to leave, the little shit hasn't moved an inch. Legs splayed out like a cowboy. Hands jammed inside his pockets. Glaring up at me with a doubtful puckered squint.

"That's it for this floor," I tell him, spinning the key on my finger. "Time for lunch."

I step around him, heading for the elevator. He bumps me with his shoulder as I pass. I let it slide and keep on walking, fighting off the urge to run. Something about him makes me nervous. Like he lives without boundaries or limits. Like he's got even less to lose than I do.

As the doors slide shut I hear him rushing after me, shouting. "Where your tools at? Where your tools at bro?"

EIGHTEEN

I make some coffee and spread the clues across the counter. The tablet is password protected. The laptop is dead and I don't have the cord. The hard drive requires a computer. The rest of Fowst's shit seems just about as promising: a black and gold cocktail napkin, a numbered cardboard ticket, the burner phone, four sales receipts and two small bags of pills.

One of the receipts is from a hardware store on Ossington. Five hundred and sixty-four dollars. No product description. Purchased on December 26th, 2017.

The other three are from a furniture store at Bathurst and Queen. Nearly fifteen thousand dollars, paid in cash on three separate dates back in January.

The ticket was issued at a pawn shop in Moss Park on February 5th. The price scrawled out across the back says $45,651. I check the calendar. February 5th was last Monday.

I open up the flip phone. Empty contact list. No photos, emails or texts. Just three numbers in the call history.

The first one goes straight to voicemail. I hang up without leaving a message.

The second number won't connect. Your call cannot be completed as dialled. Please check the number and try your call again. I do exactly what the robot lady says and it turns out she's right. The number is missing a digit.

I dial the third number.

"West Queen Spa, Ryder speaking."

I say nothing at first.

"West Queen Spa...can I help you?"

"Um, hey, it's Colin Fowst."

"Hey baby. Time for another visit?"

I mumble something that resembles yes.

"Been a while baby. Thought you might have disappeared on us or something."

"I did actually."

"Oh yeah?" she giggles. Her long fake nails punch a keyboard in the background. "Okay, I've got you in at ten with Mandy."

"Great."

"I'll be gone by then. Take care of yourself baby."

I CRAWL under my desk and lift up on the planks. I stick the hard drive, the laptop and the tablet in the cavity beneath the floor. Then I snap the flooring back in place and roll the chair on top.

I open the freezer and grab Hera's cash from inside a box of chicken fingers. I count out a thousand bucks and put it in my parka with the flip phone, the ticket and the pills. I drop the rest into a plastic bag and take it with me down the fire escape.

Zahra left the back door unlocked. I ease it open and slip inside the workshop, looking for a place to hide the cash.

Daylight leaking in through dirty windows. Workbench cluttered thick with tools. Muffled noises drifting through the ventilation system. The mundane babble of a lonely old lady. The five o'clock radio news. Zahra's voice in full retail mode, affable and quaint. I spot a gap between the air duct and the ceiling and shove the plastic bag inside.

"You know you can just use the safe, right?"

"Fuck."

Zahra's standing right behind me with her hands on her hips. I feel my face turn red.

"You're such an idiot," she laughs. "Come on."

She leads me to an alcove behind the furnace. She squats down and picks up an empty cardboard box. Hidden underneath it there's a small metal safe.

"Pretty sweet, eh? Solid steel, digital lock, eight digit pin. Got it on boxing day for like five hundred bucks."

"Couldn't someone just pick it up and walk out?"

"Maybe," she shrugs. "Weighs a couple hundred pounds though. Had to use a handcart just to get it back here. You're supposed to bolt it down I guess, but whatever. Seems pretty good like this."

The keypad beeps as she punches in the code. It buzzes and clicks and then the little door pops open. I hand her the money and she stows the bag inside. She shuts the door and waits for the beep. Then she stands back up again, dusting off her hands. Brushing past me as she leaves the room.

I follow her out into the shop. Watch her flip the sign and lock the door. Watch her draw the blinds and dim the lights and choose a playlist on her phone. She stops behind the counter, leaning on her elbows, back flat and slightly arched. Upper snaps of her denim shirt unfastened. Small firm breasts pushed together underneath.

"Beers?"

"Sure."

She comes back with two bottles and an opener. "How's life in the moving biz?"

"Total shit."

She wrinkles her nose. "Wanna come work for me?"

"The only thing I know about plants is how to smoke them."

"Yeah? Maybe I should shift production."

We both laugh. We talk about some other stuff for a bit, nothing big. Later on, I ask her what she likes about working with flowers.

"They start out in the dirt. Like I did."

"What do you mean?"

She's quiet for a moment. Staring into space. Rubbing her neck. "I'm an orphan. I mean, I was one. An orphan. As a kid. Nevermind. Anyhow, that stuff inside the safe, what's that all about dude?"

"Just a bit of cash. I'm switching banks."

She rolls her eyes and takes a drink. Disappointment lingers on her face well after she's lowered the bottle. Maybe I should have told the truth. But what exactly would I have said. That I follow people around, studying their habits, predicting their behaviour. That I make unusual deliveries. Recover valuable objects. That I pay minimal amounts of income tax. That I can take a beating?

"That bag felt pretty heavy to me."

"I've got more than one job."

"Who doesn't right?" She takes another drink. "What else do you do for work?"

"People hire me to...solve problems."

"Spooky," she grins. "What kind of problems?"

"Analog problems."

Her smile evaporates. She sets the bottle on the counter and walks slowly to the window. Arms hugged to her sides. Green eyes gazing at the street. It's dark inside the shop and getting dark outside. Cars stream south toward the highway, lighting up her face in their dull red taillight glow. After a while, she turns around.

"Can you hang out a little longer?"

I nod.

"Good. Stay here for a second."

Zahra disappears around the corner. The cooler doors swing open. The cooling system roars to life. She comes back holding a small potted plant, a white and yellow flower on a tall green stem.

"That for me?"

"Maybe," she says, sounding shy for once.

"What is it?"

"It's a lily."

"It's beautiful."

"It's one of the most common flowers in the world."

CHAPTER NINETEEN

Mist obscures the entrance to the park. I step inside and take the gravel path toward the tracks. Frozen field dappled black in bootprints. Railway lights like stains in the fog.

I lean against the dog park fence and whistle. A group of men emerges from the shadows, glowing dots of their cigarettes hovering in space. Some carry weapons. Others smirk and whisper. Once in a while, somebody laughs. They fan out and surround me and I feel the sudden urge to run.

The wall of bodies separates. Angel hobbles forward through the gap, leaning heavily on his walking stick. Tattered cloak dragging on the ground behind him. Patterned scarf wrapped tight around his face. I haven't seen his nose or mouth since the accident. No one has.

We bump fists.

I hand him the pills.

"Ever seen these before?"

He opens the bag and shakes a pill into his palm. Deep lines etched across his forehead. Pale grey eyes that almost match the fog.

"Seen em? Sure, I seen em. Can't say what they are though. One thing I do know, people can't resist this shit."

"China?"

"States."

"Opioid?"

He shakes his head. "Hospital meds. Synthetic. Junkies call it 'Truth.'"

"Who sells it?"

"Pip's the only one I know."

"Pip?"

He nods.

"And where do I find him?"

"Bloor Dufferin Towers. His crew runs the park. Mostly kids. When it's cold he stay indoors. Check the subway station or the mall."

"Dufferin Mall?"

"Yup," Angel grins, rocking and twitching and staring at the pills. "Lil bitch love the food court."

"Jesus."

"For real. Some people don't know shit about shit."

I jiggle the other bag. "How much can I get for these?"

"Five. Maybe six."

"You buying?"

He takes out a tarnished silver money clip, peeling off fifties and twenties.

"Make it two hundred."

He gives me a look. "Yo—you sure?"

"Absolutely."

"Respects bro," he says, handing me the cash. "Can you grab any more of this shit?"

"I'll try and dig something up."

He takes the pills and ambles back toward his flock. They gather in a loose formation and descend into the railway corridor, footsteps replacing a farewell.

I find a bench with a view and light a joint. The wind strengthens and the fog clears and soon I'm alone beneath the moon and the stars.

Looking east across the tracks, the city is a photograph. A postcard sent by tourists. A dream or a promise or a curse. A place to find yourself, reveal yourself, to drown yourself in something vast. Every window is at least one person. Every building is a light that won't go out. Who owns this view. How many millions is it worth. How many evictions made space for all this money?

CHAPTER
TWENTY

The spa is obviously a rub and tug. Dingy narrow staircase to the plaza's second floor. Thick steel door painted pink. I ring the bell and wait. The peephole darkens.

"Yeah?"

"Hey it's Colin. I'm here to see Mandy."

"I'm Mandy."

Fuck.

I hold up a handful of cash. "How bout it?"

"Fine," she says, unlocking the door. "Come on in."

I follow her inside. Dark brown tan. Straight blonde hair bleached blonder. Tight black shorts that only cover half her ass. A little past her prime but still a lot better than most.

She leads me through the lobby to a small dim room that smells like testicles and sun tan lotion. Peeling beige counter with a bar sized sink. Textbooks stacked beside a picture frame. A humidifier pumps out thin white vapour and the air feels moist and gross.

She washes her hands and lays a towel on the massage table. Bruises on her neck. Track marks on her forearms. Gold and silver stars tattooed across her back.

"It's fifty bucks for thirty minutes," she says in her dull brassy voice, "or eighty for the hour."

"That's not the reason that I'm here."

She puts her hands on my chest and shoves me back onto the table. "Most guys change their minds toward the end."

"I'll pay you for the hour if I can ask a couple questions."

She pulls her hair into a ponytail and wiggles in between my thighs, leaning forward till we're almost cheek to cheek. She smells like cheap shampoo and lip gloss.

"We have to at least do something," she whispers. "He's watching us."

"Who's watching?"

Her eyes dart toward a camera on the wall above the door.

"Who's watching? You can tell me."

"Please," she says, handing me a towel. "Don't make things any worse."

She turns around and tells me to undress. I hang my clothes behind the door and wrap the towel around my waist. She lays another towel on the table, smoothing it with her fingers, glancing up at the camera. "Cash first."

I hand her two fifties. She sticks the money in a change purse on the counter. I lie down on my stomach and she gets to work.

"Does that camera have audio?"

"No, too old. It just does black and white video."

"Why so careful then?"

Mandy squirts some oil onto my back. I watch her shadow through the face hole in the table. The supple arch above her buttocks. The buxom wobble of her breasts.

"The name," she sighs. "Why did you use his name to book your appointment?"

"I'm looking for him."

"Everyone is looking for him."

"Why?"

"He comes by a couple times a month," she says, still whispering. "He was supposed to come last week, but he never showed."

"So what? I don't get it. "

She stops rubbing and steps away from the table. I roll over and sit up straight. "Don't worry. I'm not a cop."

"He doesn't come here for the girls. He comes with pills. For Dima."

"Who's Dima?"

She hesitates.

I reach out and grab her wrist. "Tell me. Right now. Who is Dima?"

Then the lights go out and Mandy starts screaming.

CHAPTER TWENTY-ONE

E very morning Angel kept his meds beneath his tongue. When the nurses left he'd use his breakfast tray to break the pills in half. Then he'd start making trades. Salt and vinegar potato chips. Chocolate flavoured protein bars. Apple fritters in a clear plastic wrapper. After lock-up he'd crush the rest and snort the powder through a straw. Then he'd kneel beside the door, watching television through the slot, singing along with the music videos until someone told him to shut up. At night he'd stay awake for hours, sitting on the metal stool that was welded to the metal table, tattooing himself with crayon ink and a staple he pried out of a magazine and sharpened on the waist-high wall around the shower. Outside he'd use twigs to drag cigarette butts through the fence that stood between the prison yard and the parking lot where the guards took their breaks. He showered once a week and hoarded dirty laundry and not one person sent him money or drove up for a visit. His father was an alcoholic who got laid off from a paper mill. His mother was a schizophrenic who rarely left the house. He wore thrift shop clothes to school and stole candy from the corner store just to have some food inside his lunchbox. He had never travelled or even left the city limits and by sixteen he was fucked for life. He was short and loud and stupid and he almost always smelled like shit. But for what seemed like a very long time, Angel was my only friend.

That summer the cellblock went on strike. One hundred and twenty inmates against twelve white guards. The whole thing started over food. Somebody found bugs in their soup and everyone went apeshit all at once. We flipped the big steel food cart and barricaded the front door. We flung water bottles at the lights until we broke out all the bulbs. We started little fires with magazines and newspapers. We clogged the main toilet with shoes and balled-up shirts and flooded the range with smelly grey water.

The guards cut the power and by the afternoon it was hot as hell in there. We stripped down to our boxers and waded through the sewage to stay cool. Altogether, there were twenty guys on the range. We had enough food to last about a day and a half.

By the third day things had gotten pretty desperate. Everybody with a main floor cell crammed onto the catwalk when the toilet water breached the bottom bunks. Fights broke out over food and matches and cigarettes. Everyone was off their meds. The phones didn't work and the guys with wives and kids were beginning to crack. Around dusk we spotted the swat team getting ready in the bubble. Gas masks, riot shields, batons. Pepper spray and rubber bullets and a water cannon.

The biggest fucker on the range got up and ambled down the staircase. Everybody stopped and watched.

He waded over and stood beside the showers. Then he wound up and drove his foot into the corner of the privacy wall. The whole thing seemed to vibrate for a second. On his second kick a hairline crack appeared in the mortar that anchored the upper row of blocks. That's all it took to get us on our feet, bouncing shirtless down the metal steps, splashing across the range, stomping down the wall with wild insurgent fury. The pounding got so loud the SWAT team heard it from the bubble. We could see them through the glass, rushing to get ready. Strapping on their gear as the captain barked his final orders.

It only took ten minutes to bring the wall down. After it collapsed we worked in groups, dropping big chunks onto little chunks, making blocks that were small enough to throw. Even Angel joined in, gathering rocks in an orange cotton bag he fashioned from a t-shirt. By the time the battering ram first struck the door, we were armed with fist-sized concrete bricks.

The flash bomb caught the range off-guard. People screaming, bodies splashing to the ground. They fired the rubber bullets next. I heard them zipping through the air above me. The cops pounced on anyone that dropped. Held their heads underwater. Slapped restraints around their wrists and ankles. Dragged them out into the bubble and dumped them in a filthy crowded cell.

Not everyone got hit. It was a full blown riot and the charges would be heavy. There was no point in going down without a fight. We crouched behind our mattresses, collecting broken concrete, building up our last defence. The cops picked up their riot shields and got into formation. Gas masks blacking out their faces. Tapping their batons in rhythm like some fascist's fever dream.

They marched onto the range and ducked behind the shields. Before the gas could be deployed, we leapt to our feet and pelted them with bricks. Angel led the way, darting from our makeshift bunker, whipping stones between the shields. Veering closer with every pass. Daring them to take him down.

I was first to spot the water cannon.

I yelled but way too late.

Angel ran into the open and leapt high into the air. As the brick left his hand, two of the cops stepped sideways, water blasting out between them like a missile.

The burst hit Angel squarely in the chest. Flying backwards, pummelled by the spray. Cartwheeling head over feet. He landed mouth first, on a jagged concrete stump protruding from the broken shower wall. Face crushed against the brick like a pile of uncooked meat.

CHAPTER
TWENTY-TWO

I slip to the floor and roll under the table. Blows rain down like thunder, hammering the padding above me. It's pitch black and I'm naked and Mandy's screaming somewhere in the dark.

"SHUT UP BITCH."

His shout shakes the walls. Mandy's screams become muffled sobs. In the silence, I hear him panting, catching his breath. He's standing right beside me.

I drive my heel into his knee. His leg buckles and he falls. A second later, I'm on top of him, kneeling on his chest, reaching for his neck so I can strangle him or choke him out. He flails his arms, wooden bat clattering against the floor. His coat is thick and damp, like the hide of some huge animal. And every time I think I've found his neck my fingers just slip further up the leather.

He bucks me off and swings the bat into my face. Bright lights burst inside my head. Cold saliva pours into my mouth. I crawl away, aiming for Mandy's sobs, trying not to puke. I grab the sink and pull myself upright. The bat crashes off the counter near my fingers. I drop down and crawl beneath the table.

Nothing happens at first. Then I hear him slowly turn around, creeping closer. Tracking odours in the dark. I get up on my hands and knees. He takes another step. I kick out hard, but my foot doesn't connect. He leaps and throws his weight onto the table and it breaks and collapses down on top of me.

Arms pinned to my sides. Legs limp and useless. I can feel his hot breath on my skin. I can smell his drugstore aftershave. He starts to get up and when he shifts his weight, I can't help but groan.

He freezes, listening. Then he slides his hand across the padding, feeling with this fingers for the face hole. And then he's touching me. He's grunting and wheezing and fingering my face.

I hear the wood slip through his hands as he plows the bat into my nose. Blood pours out in rhythmic spurts. I wait for THE SURGE. But it never happens when I need it. And for the first time in years, I feel truly afraid.

He hits me again. A flap of skin tears off my forehead and folds over my eye. "EAT IT CUNT," he shouts.

And his voice is shallow and empty and cold. Unlike anything I've ever heard before. It's not the voice of a man. It's the voice of a God or a beast. Then he rams the bat into the hole and I'm gone.

CHAPTER
TWENTY-THREE

I wake up with my head inside a toilet. Mandy's kneeling next to me, cleaning out my wounds. When the bleeding stops she puts a bandage on my face and tells me I should see a doctor. We both know I can't do that, but she says it anyway.

I flush the toilet and get on my feet. Puke in the sink. Bloody trail of footprints smeared across the clean white bathroom floor.

"That my blood?"

"Obviously," she says, taking my arm. "Your forehead's a mess. You've got a bad concussion too."

"Where are we?"

"My place. You'll be safe here, for now at least."

She walks me to the bedroom and helps me into bed. She pours a glass of water from a fancy silver jug. She rifles through the nightstand drawer, then reaches out with a small red pill on the tip of her finger.

"I'm gonna go clean up," she says, putting her finger in my mouth. "This will make everything better, I promise."

· · ·

MANDY UNDRESSES IN THE SHADOWS. She brushes her hair in front of the mirror then strides across the bedroom like she's wading into the ocean.

The pain in my head is gone. The sheets feel cool against my skin. I'm buzzing and weightless and free. In another world, the same way I felt outside the diner.

She climbs onto the bed. Crawling up the mattress on her hands and knees, ass lifted, breasts grazing softly up my thighs. She lingers near my waist. We lock eyes for a moment. And then I'm lost inside the world of her mouth.

I watch her head bob up and down. I count the stars tattooed across her back. I grab her by the hair and she moans and goes deeper and slower. After a while, she comes up for air.

"What's your real name anyway?"

I say nothing.

She sits up, straddling my waist. "Come on. You can tell me."

"I can't."

She slides her hips backward, grinding on me slowly, touching herself. "Please?"

I hold out for as long as I can. And then I tell her. I tell her my real name. I tell her my name and she puts me inside and then it's happening. And she's soaked and tight and smooth. And I'm delirious. Sinking through the mattress. White light fills the room and there's nothing in the world except her body, taut and quivering above me. She leans back and puts her hands on my shins, riding me harder and faster. I steel myself, bearing down. Ready for the end. She throws back her head and bellows my name. Hot thin fluid surges out of her in waves. And every writhing spasm feels like freedom.

. . .

After we fuck we smoke a joint in bed. Mandy lying with me in the dark. Golden body partly covered by the sheet. City lights painting black and yellow patterns on the wall.

"Hope we didn't wake your son."

She sits up and makes a face. "I don't have a son."

"That kid. In the photo at the spa?"

"On the countertop? Who knows. Probably came with the frame. We use that stuff to get better tips. Same thing with the textbooks."

"Clever."

"That's one way to put it. Pretty shitty if you think about it."

"There's shittier things to think about."

"True," she takes a drag. "Whatever though, I'm almost outta there."

"Changing jobs?"

"Changing jobs," she passes me the joint, "changing cities, changing everything I hope."

"Won't it be weird for you, living somewhere else?"

"Not for me. I'm not even from here."

"Windsor?"

"Michigan. Followed my boyfriend up here a couple years ago. Pretty dumb thing to do, right? But I was young, you know? Anyway so of course we break up like a year later and I don't have the money to move back home. So I went to work at a couple different places. All of them were terrible, by the way. But I survived. And then this job came along and it was on the streetcar line and they always paid in cash and boom. That was that. And I guess I just got used to the money. Got lazy. Know what I mean?"

"Absolutely."

"Anyway, fuck it. Time for me to go. I mean it's not like it's even that good here."

"It used to be."

"Did it?"

"Yeah," I tell her. But I'm not even sure if I'm right.

"Well, regardless, the winters here really suck. And there's still so many things I want to do with my life."

"Like what?"

Mandy lays back and shuts her eyes and recites a list of impossible desires. A vapid bourgeois fantasy where life is one long trip to the mall. And I can't help but envy her optimism. Her magical thinking. Her naive sense of hope and certainty.

"When do you leave town?"

"Soon. Already gave my two weeks notice at the spa. Plus, I finally had some good luck. So I'm set for a few months when it comes to money. Still got some stuff to do before I hit the road, packing, errands, shit like that. Also I'm working this stupid party Sunday night. I was gonna bail at first, but the money's just too good not to stick around."

"Maybe I'll see you again before you go."

She smiles and rests her head against my chest.

"Maybe you will."

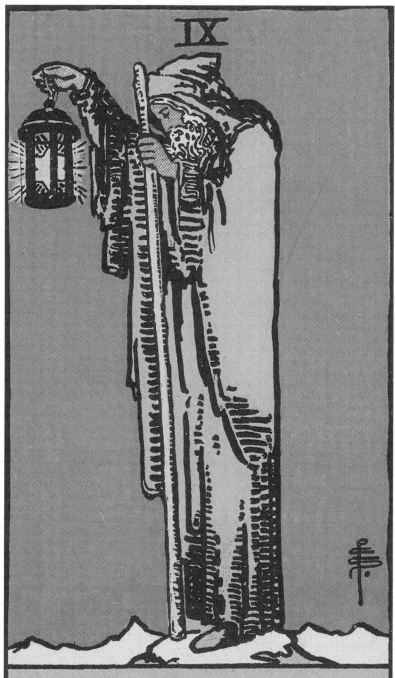

SATURDAY

CHAPTER
TWENTY-FOUR

Mandy's gone when I wake up. I roll onto her side of the bed and lay there for a while, half asleep, half dreaming about spending the day with her. Let's order breakfast and watch a movie in bed. Let's shower and change and go for a drive. Rosedale. Forest Hill. The Bridle Path. Let's park and walk and marvel at the fortune that surrounds us, at this wealth we'll never touch. Let's mourn the dreams we had when we were young. Before we learned how money works. Before we knew we were slaves.

"WENT OUT for food and coffee. Be back soon."

I drop her note and swing my legs onto the floor. My jeans look pretty good but both my shirts are drenched in blood. There's a bathrobe in a ball on the floor. I throw it on and take a look around.

Mandy's place is a one bedroom condo down on Richmond Street. Brown plastic floor that looks like wood. White plastic couch that looks like leather. Floor to ceiling windows facing west.

What a view. Thirty, maybe forty stories up. From this height and distance, I see everything I knew deep down was true. I see parks on high rise rooftops. I see tents in every park. I see whole neighbourhoods acquired by modern feudalists. Little Portugal. Little Italy. Dufferin Grove. Stout brick bungalows, built by hand, sold in seconds and demolished in days. Replaced by million dollar craters. New places to plant capital. New tombs to bury wealth.

How much money can a place absorb before it becomes a caricature, a karaoke version of itself?

What happens when a city exists in memory alone?

What will four more years deliver?

Glass box smart homes, replicating on an exponential curve. Front lawn shrubbery trimmed by licensed estheticians. Patio furniture sent by courier to heated indoor storage. Household pets wearing winter boots and coats.

City of stagnant taxes. City of laundered money. City of well-housed technocrats, buoyed by inherited wealth. Inhabiting a parallel world.

It's almost ten and Mandy's still not home. There's food in the fridge and tea and coffee in the cupboard. And I get the feeling that she won't be coming back at all. And if she does, she may not be alone.

I take a shower and search the bedroom for a shirt that fits. The dresser drawers are empty. Same thing goes for the closet.

Does Mandy even live here?

Does anyone?

I pop my head inside the den. Long wool coat folded on a chair. Black and gold gown on a hook behind the door. On the floor beneath the desk, a pair of black stiletto heels, unworn and expensive. There's a pale pink suitcase with a matching pink duffle bag. I unzip the suitcase and spread it open on the carpet. I find a t-shirt she probably uses for pyjamas. It smells okay. I put it on and start looking for a pair of socks.

I turn the duffle upside down and dump the contents on the floor. Tampons. Hair straightener. Make-up in a little zippered pouch. Bras and panties, track pants and jeans, a weird package wrapped in butcher paper and tied shut with twine.

I pick it up. It weighs a ton. I set it down and work on loosening the knot. It's a black velvet case with a yellow note stuck to the top: "Now we're even. Call me once you cross the border. ~C"

I slowly lift the lid. The inner case is lined in silk, with a pair of quilted cavities positioned side by side like twins. One of the spots is empty. The other one contains an over-sized antique key.

I take it out and hold it up and it glitters in my hand like a tiny star, too bright and heavy to be anything but gold.

I wipe it with my shirt and put it back inside the case. The key feels rough against my palm. I take a closer look and there's a small engraving stamped into the handle:

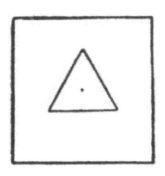

CHAPTER
TWENTY-FIVE

The streetcars are down. They're running shuttles across Queen. I step on board and pay the fare and join the crowd near the back. We lurch out into traffic. Frost creeping up the windows. Engine whining in the cold. The other riders look sullen and dirty and tired. Beaten down by thankless work. Coated in psychosocial ash. In the ads above the windowpanes, a young couple of unidentifiable ethnicity embrace on their newly purchased veranda. Freedom Is A Variable Rate Mortgage From Royal Dominion Bank.

I find a place to point my eyes. I slip my hand into my pocket and rest my fingers on the key. I think about getting paid.

The bus stops hard at Bay Street, engulfed by an ocean of people. Hundreds, maybe thousands, cascading down the steps of old city hall. Waving flags and wearing vests. Faceless angry people clutching phones.

They surround the bus. Banging on the windows and tearing at the doors. The suspension creaks as we lurch from side to side and I imagine the bus tipping over and the mob barging in and tearing us apart.

The other riders don't seem to notice. A fat man does a crossword and cleans his ears with his finger. An old lady falls asleep against the window, purse held tightly in her lap. The rest of them gawk at their phone screens like stupid children, swiping and scrolling through American news.

Police arrive on horseback. Helicopters echo in the sky. The mob loses interest in the bus and joins a larger group coalescing further down the road. Their leader shouts a rhyming slogan through a megaphone. Her disciples chant and shake their fists. They unfurl a yellow banner and stretch it out across the intersection.

Reporters settle into place. The crowd counts backwards from ten. Three! Two! One! They pose in triumph as the street catches fire, immolated by the white hot blaze of camera flash.

The media seems satisfied. The protest thins. Our bus resumes its route. Paramedics sit on gurneys smoking cigarettes. The fire department collects donations of canned food and gently used toys. Policemen hand out coupons for rotisserie chicken.

The demonstrators filter back into the city. Lined up for gourmet burgers, rushing off to brunch, safely stowed inside a coffee shop resting blistered feet and thumbs. New activists of Toronto, raging adjacent to the machine. I used to be one of these people. Before outrage was a corporate asset. Before identity was just a meme. I was one of them. Now I ride the bus.

CHAPTER
TWENTY-SIX

The pawnshop is a redbrick rathole south of Queen and Jarvis. Buzzer system at the entrance. Bulletproof shield around the cash. Inventory like a garbage dump for impulse purchases. Night vision goggles. Vacuum cleaner robots. Infomercial pressure cooker pots.

The guy behind the counter doesn't bother with hello. Wire frame glasses. Crew cut. Faded khaki army surplus shirt.

I tap on the glass.

He looks up from his paper.

"Ya?"

I slide the ticket through the slot. "Need some help with this."

"It's a piece of paper buddy. Not sure what else to say."

"Why don't you start with anything at all?"

"We're not really in the helping business," he says, rolling his eyes. "If you wanna buy something, I can help you with that."

I push a fifty at him. He pockets the money and clears his throat. "Tell me again what you're trying to figure out?"

"I need to find out what was pawned, but I can't read the handwriting."

"That's Pauly," he snorts. "I don't even think he can read it sometimes."

"Can you show me the item?"

"Can I show you the item?"

I nod at the crap-filled rack behind him. "Must be here somewhere, right?"

"Pal, this is a receipt. That thing is long gone."

"I don't follow."

"When you pawn something here, we give you one of these." He holds up a bright orange tag. "This," he taps the counter, "is a receipt." He slides it back through the slot. My fifty bucks stays firmly in his pocket. "Get it now boss? Your guy repaid the loan. He bought his stuff back."

CHAPTER TWENTY-SEVEN

Dufferin Mall seems imported from the suburbs. Whitby or Milton or Vaughan, not some random west end neighbourhood. Last minute vacations. Last year's fashions. Last night's donuts. A store that only sells luggage. Free wifi and air conditioning for the latchkey kids in the housing blocks across the road.

The girl snaps the lid onto my coffee. "That's him over there, lined up at the smoothie place. Little guy in the baseball cap."

I drop a twenty on the counter and tell her she can keep the change. Take a seat. Deal myself a hand of solitaire, keeping watch.

Pip swaggers through the foodcourt like a shitty prince. Swinging one arm, basically limping. When his pants get low he grabs his belt to hold them up. Long white t-shirt. Clunky unlaced boots. Chains in golden layers around his neck.

He sits down at a table. Sucking on his drink and playing with his phone. Every thirty minutes a runner makes a drop. Free newspapers, dusty paperbacks, other mundane objects stuffed with money. High school kids, fourteen or fifteen years old, blending in with the Friday evening crowd. The system seems amateurish, almost comical. Like something copied from a movie. But the whole mall seems that way to me.

This goes on all night. Pip never moves. I watch him sit there, collecting money. Watch him squint and slouch and adjust his balls. Watch him stare at other people as if they're replicated objects, two dimensional characters in a movie or a game. I study his blankness. His lack of self. He becomes who the moment demands. And when the moment ends, he's nobody.

Custodians appear pushing floor mopping machines. Shopkeepers pull down their gates. A recorded voice announces that the mall will close in thirty minutes.

I head outside and move the van a little closer to the entrance. Then I sit and wait and go over the plan. Any minute, Pip will leave the mall, heading for the park across the street. That's when I'll start tailing him.

I'll run up from behind and hit him in the head. If he doesn't drop, I'll hit him again. Then I'll drag him somewhere dark, the trees or the bushes or in between the dumpsters. I'll take his gun and shove the barrel down his throat. Rough him up a bit. Find out what he knows. Knock him out and rob him blind.

Pip strolls outside just after nine, already smoking a cigarette. Big red headphones, hands and body moving with the music. He takes out his phone and taps the screen and a few minutes later a little white hatchback stops at the curb. He waves and climbs inside. I start the engine and hit the gas, hoping we aren't going very far. Father charged me fifty dollars for the van but he never mentioned the half empty tank.

The hatchback exits the lot. I stay two cars back and follow them south. They make a left at Dundas Street, heading east toward the core. We catch a red at Ossington and coast to a stop. Bars and restaurants at full capacity. Picture windows like billboard ads for money. Long haired businessmen. Tall blonde women wearing short tight skirts. Bright young people with extra time and extra friends, all their petty celebrations.

The light turns green. We roll ahead. Beaconsfield, Palmerston, other fake neighbourhoods named by realtors; Trinity Bellwoods, fully gentrified and lame, trust fund poets, state sponsored musicians; Kensington Market, Upper Chinatown, sidewalk vegetables, curbside garbage, windows fringed in duck; Grange Park, University Avenue, Bay Street, nothing to see here, come back Monday morning; Yonge-Dundas Square, placarded zealots, polite agnostics, overdressed suburbanites, lined up at the theatre, choking on electric light.

I follow them through Regent Park. They hang a right on River Street and roll south for a block until they pull into the driveway of the animal shelter.

I turn the van around and park it up the road. Leave the engine running. Hurry down the sidewalk to the shelter.

A car door slams. Someone bangs on a window. A heavy door creaks open and shut.

I slip behind the hatchback. The driver's watching something on his phone. I duck into the shadows. Shoulder pressed against the building wall. Crouched and creeping closer to the entrance.

I peer into the lobby through a crack in the blinds. Pip's standing at the welcome desk leaning on his elbows. Puffy red coat. Black jeans hanging off his ass. He must be robbing the place. Fentanyl. Tranquilizers. Puppies.

A middle-aged woman meets him at the desk. Canvas shoes. Pale green scrubs. Plain-faced and tired and meekly holding a small white dog. Shitzu. Maybe a terrier.

Pip claps his hands and the little dog races through the lobby and leaps into his arms, licking his face and pawing at his neck and chest. He cradles the dog like a baby, laughing and twirling in a circle. The woman watches from a distance with her arms folded on her chest. Sad reluctant smile. Premature lines around her nose and eyes and mouth. Pip twirls toward the window and I recognize his face. It's the same kid that banged on Fowst's apartment door.

Pip says something to the woman but I can't quite hear him through the glass. She crosses the room. He hands her an envelope. She tears it open. It's a birthday card. He's expecting a reaction but her expression doesn't change. She looks uncomfortable. She hasn't spoken yet at all.

There's a long awkward silence. Pip points toward the exit and leans in for a hug. The woman seems willing but recoils as he nears, shrinking back like she's disgusted by his touch.

He lunges out and grabs her wrist. She shrieks and wriggles free, retreating across the room, white shoes squeaking on the floor.

Pip takes his time. Hurling abuse as he slowly closes in. She seems pummelled by his voice. Absorbing words like punches. Bound to him by invisible chains. The dog cowers underneath the lobby furniture, back legs trembling in a fresh puddle of piss. The woman spots the dog and something happens. Her face changes, enkindled by the cruel potential of a phrase. Her gaze sharpens. Her mouth twists. Her eyes gleam as her lips deploy the taunt. Brief and brutal, honed for years to geld his outsized ego.

For a moment, no one moves. They glare like silent maniacs, faces moist, chests heaving. Then Pip explodes. He reaches up and slams her head into the wall. She staggers sideways. Smashed face buried in her hands. Fresh blood spurting out between her fingers. He snags her hair and pulls her close and whispers softly in her ear. She shuts her eyes, nodding yes until he's finished. He lets her go and she tries to run but her legs go limp and she tumbles to the floor. Prostrated on the dusty granite, sobbing and broken.

Pip stands over her, grinning. He holds up a handful of cash, counting off bills with the flick of his thumb. The money flutters down and settles on her face. Glued in place by tears and blood.

Satisfied, he swaggers to the door. I leap to my feet and race back up the road. The hatchback circles the round-about and pulls into the street. I jump behind the wheel and stomp the gas, merging crudely into traffic, heading south toward the lake. No sign of Pip's ride anywhere. Hardly any action in the dreary condo grotto where King and River Street collide.

I cut through the Distillery District, racing west across Mill Street. I catch the light at Cherry Street and spot the hatchback three cars down the line. We pass beneath the Gardiner's rusty ribs and weave between its maze of pillars and roll across the old steel bridge. To where the city ends.

TWENTY-EIGHT

We used to get lost down here. Over the drawbridge that sways in the wind. Past the foundry and the pier and the smoke stacks of the decommissioned power plant.

Along brown sandy spits. Ducks paddling in the shallows. Bullfrogs croaking in the grass. Reclaimed swamp land, filled in over decades by machines. Dead livestock. Animal waste. Plumes of downtown sewage, coalescing in the bogs. Garbage land, jutting out into the harbour like a hangnail.

But city council made a deal. New bridges, new islands, new pharmacies and coffee shops.

Who will remember the land as it was?

As it might have been?

This last neglected place. Unmolested by developers. Quiet home to our itinerant creatures. Expropriated by corporations. Colonized by condo towers.

Smart buildings. Smart streets. Smart trash cans and crosswalks. A high-tech waterfront community constructed on peninsulas of corpses and shit. The inevitable convergence of raw sewage and investment capital.

Welcome to Toronto's next great neighbourhood.
Welcome to The Port Lands.

CHAPTER
TWENTY-NINE

The hatchback stops at the nightclub on the pier. Low dingy warehouse sprawling out along the shore. Giant rooftop billboard lighting up the ice. A neon yellow wheel of fortune, spinning clockwise with terrible velocity.

I kill the lights and park the van. The club won't open for at least another hour. But Pip's not here to dance. He's waiting for someone.

He climbs the steps and lights a cigarette. Stubborn angry posture that reminds me of the past. Chest pushed out. Head leaned back. Staring across the harbour, smoking. Nothing to worry about. Nothing to lose. A self made man child. Violent and simple.

Headlights flicker on the road. A white rental van cuts across the parking lot. It skids around a streetlight and stops below the steps. Windows belching vape smoke. Bass drum rattling the bumper.

Pip takes one last haul on his cigarette. He jogs down the steps and hops inside. The van slams into gear and speeds away, music thumping, back wheels flinging gravel.

I follow them further south, over the second bridge, city

bottom, dark and flat like driving out onto the ice, down-town fading slowly in the rearview, road signs plowed under in the ditch, wet snow flung like mud behind the van.

They stop at the container yard on Unwin Street. I coast past and pull onto the shoulder. Kill the headlights. Leave the engine running. Cross the ditch and walk north along the fence. Ships moored in darkness at the terminal. Smell of diesel fuel and sewage. The lake's strange nocturnal glow.

Lights off inside the office building. No cars in the exec-utive lot. I stick to the ditch, away from the security cameras, heading for the driveway and the entrance to the yard. Containers stacked like city blocks behind the fence. Tire tracks leading south toward the gate.

Bright lights flicker in the gatehouse window. I crouch down, approaching slowly, staying out of sight. A short staircase leads up to the door. I climb the first step and peer over the window ledge. The guard is slouched over in his chair, fast asleep in front of a television set.

I squeeze between the gates and hurry down the makeshift road. The streetlights wane. The gatehouse shrinks behind me. The containers start to change. Roofs caved in, sides torn open, an obsolete city swapped out for something new.

I follow the road to a wide flat clearing, a junkyard in the centre of the lot. Slabs of broken concrete. Old dead cars without doors or seats or windows. Family boats on crippled trailers, hulls bleached white by the sun.

Headlights shine like halos in the distance. I slink ahead. Hunkered like a soldier, navigating the debris. I spot the rental van straddling an access road near the southernmost fence. I duck behind an oil drum and peer around the side. Flickering light on a crooked wooden pole. The lake concealed in darkness in the space beyond the fence. Two new containers positioned side by side like twins, jet black and spotless.

Pip's leaned up against the van smoking a cigarette. The driver's talking on his cellphone, shuffling his feet to stay warm. Black leather coat with the collar popped. Thick beard trimmed to stubble. Full red lips, pouty and feminine. Tattoos on the backside of his hand. He ends the call and slides his keys across the hood.

Pip makes the catch with both hands, cigarette dangling from his lips. "What are these for?"

"Open the containers," the driver says, unbuckling his belt. "I need to piss."

Pip fumbles with the locks. Shoulders tense. Hands shaking in the cold. He seems uncomfortable, even nervous. I feel nervous too.

The driver holds his dick in one hand and his vape pen in the other. He sighs loudly, vaping and pissing and farting. Steam rising from the puddle mixes with the flavoured mist drifting from his nose.

Pip unlocks the doors and turns around. The driver shakes himself for a long time, fishing for a compliment. Pip keeps his eyes down. "Now what?"

"Go ahead. Look inside."

Pip takes a step, then hesitates. "For real?"

"Go on, my friend. You have earned it, yes?"

Pip shrugs and heaves backward on the door. "I can't see."

"There is switch, on wall."

Lights blaze inside the container. The driver, now a silhouette, sucks his vape and waits. Pip saunters back outside, astonished.

"Holy shit!"

The driver takes out a banana. "So," he says, removing the peel. "And what do you think?"

"Bro—all that shit's for Sunday night?"

The driver mumbles yes between bites.

"Unreal," Pip says, snapping his fingers quickly.

"Come over here, my friend. I have something else to show you."

Pip shrugs and moves a few steps closer. The driver pulls a black and silver pistol from his coat.

"Wait, wait," Pip stutters, backing up. "Hang on a minute bro."

The driver lays the gun flat in his palm. "Go on. Take it."

"You serious?"

"Of course, my friend."

Pip grins and takes the gun. He shuts one eye, lining up the sights, aiming at imaginary targets like a kid playing cops and robbers.

The driver stands and watches, smiling thinly, with a twinkle in his eye that wasn't there before.

Pip spins the gun on his index finger and shoves it in his jacket pocket. "Yo," he says, reaching out for a handshake. "I just gotta say, thanks for everything bro."

The driver smiles and spreads his arms. "Come here!"

Pip steps into the embrace and they grunt and slap each other's backs like frat boys at a kegger.

"Okay, I'm good," Pip squirms. But the driver's grip only tightens. "Bro what the fuck?"

The driver jams a syringe into Pip's neck. He stumbles away, moaning and clutching his throat. His legs go limp and he sinks to the ground, eyes rolled back, foam leeching from his mouth, yellow brown stains seeping from his jeans into the snow. And then the tremors, like electric shocks. Last jolts of life leaving the body.

I turn away for a moment. I've never watched someone die. And suddenly Pip seems like a lost little boy. A soot covered orphan from some old story. Icy blue eyes, colder now. Focussed on my hiding place as if he saw me crouching here as he was dying.

The driver kicks the corpse and steps away. Nothing happens. He squats and checks it for a pulse, vaping and humming a tune. Then he takes the gun from Pip's coat and puts it in a big clear plastic bag.

Distant growl of an engine. Tires crunching on the unplowed road. The driver stands and shields his eyes. The big car rolls to a stop, grille aimed squarely at my spot behind the drum. The front door opens. Sturdy legs swing out. Tactical boots. Navy blue trousers with thin red stripes. The engine shuts off and then the headlights too. Dark black tinted windows. Plain steel rims. It's not a car. It's a silver SUV.

"Dead yet?"

The driver kicks the body. "He is now dead."

"Get his prints?"

The driver tosses him the bag. The cop pockets the gun and rests his hands on his hips. "Come on," he sighs. "Let's get this done. You've got somewhere else to be."

He takes off his jacket and pulls on a pair of latex gloves. They grab Pip's wrists and ankles, shuffling sideways toward the containers. They put him down and take a rest. Then they pick him up again, swinging him back and forth, counting out loud as the body gains momentum. On three, they heave him inside like roadkill. "You need to be more careful," the cop says, peeling off his gloves. "I'm sick of cleaning up your mess."

I focus on his voice, listening for something that might help me later on. But he speaks like someone broadcasting the news. Universal diction, without a trace of any accent. From everywhere and nowhere all at once.

The driver puffs his vape and shrugs. "I am also cleaning mess, no?"

The cop spits a wad of phlegm into the dark. "Fuck. Never mind. You find the other one yet?"

"No," the driver slumps. "Not yet. And I am sorry, but this fucking guy, I swear. He's fucking with us. I'm telling you—something here is very fucked up."

The cop takes his coat and marches back toward the vehicle. He opens the door and stands on the gunnel and his face catches the light. Light grey bangs cut straight across his forehead. Beady eyes jammed too close together. Royal blue maple leaf tattooed on his left arm.

"Except, he's not fucking with me, is he?" the cop shouts. "I'll be just fine. I'm not drowning in debt. I'm not out here violating my parole. I'm in total control of my body and mind. I'm a golden fucking God. So, my stupid friend, if he's fucking with someone, he must be fucking with you, right? Cause he's sure as shit not fucking with me."

The driver bows his head, silent and ashamed.

"No more excuses," the cop booms from above the unmarked cruiser. "Find him by Sunday, or you can take his place."

The cop gets in and drives away. The driver trudges through the snow, muttering and locking the container doors. He climbs into the van and turns the key. As the drone of the engine fades, I swear I can hear Pip, still alive, flopping like a dying fish in the container.

CHAPTER
THIRTY

I catch up with the rental van heading west on Lakeshore Boulevard. Oldies on the radio. Lit joint burning in the ash tray. Wiper blades keeping time. It's getting late and the roads are mostly empty. He's in the slow lane, cruising just above the limit, periodic vape smoke bursting from the driver-side window.

Maybe you take it easy after a murder. Contemplate the consequences. Concoct a strong defence. Plan a foolproof getaway, fake passports, foreign bank accounts, private jets. Something tells me it wasn't his first time. Or his second or his third time either. Everything looked too routine. Stick the kid, dump the body, drive away. Like changing a tire or taking out the trash. And his weird dynamic with the cop. Neutered and servile. Chained to another man's power.

I want nothing to do with these people. But here I am, only witness to an execution, tailing the killer across town. Sucked into the future by a pile of dirty money and a dead boy in a box.

The van signals right and heads north up Jameson. We take a left at King Street and roll west toward St. Joseph's

Hospital. He hangs a hard right on Sunnyside and coasts slowly through the shipping paddock gates.

I park in the visitor's lot and circle back on foot. Snow swirling thickly in the updraft. Tractor trailer up on blocks. One small light above each loading dock, darkness everywhere else.

A door creaks open somewhere deep inside the paddock. I duck into the shadows between the trailer and the fence. Broken warehouse pallets. Shattered glass. Shredded litter mounded up by rodents or the wind.

I shuffle along the length of the trailer and peek around the tailgate. White van parked against the hospital wall, hidden from the cameras by a dumpster. There's an exit door propped open with a broomstick and a pile of cardboard boxes stacked high inside the doorway.

The driver moves with an urgency that was absent at the yard. Jacket off. Sleeves pushed up. Orthodox cross bouncing off his chest as he rushes boxes from the building to the van. Three horizontal bars instead of just one. And that weird bottom bar, so short and crooked.

The final box won't fit inside the van. He shoves it in a couple different ways, then shrugs and heaves it up into the dumpster. He walks back to the van and opens the passenger door and grabs a pack of tissues from the glovebox. Sopping sweat off his face and neck, humming the same stupid tune. Pausing every now and then to suck his vape and look at his phone.

That's when I remember the burner phone. I dig it out and turn it on, scrolling through the call history, hoping that my hunch pays off. The first number was the spa. I try the second number, but it still won't connect. I dial the third number.

A ringtone echoes through the paddock. The driver

freezes, staring at his screen in disbelief. He answers on the sixth ring.

"Yes?"

I stay quiet.

"Hello? Hello?"

I say nothing again.

"Who's there?"

I decide to take a chance.

"Dima?"

"What?"

"Is this Dima?"

Silence.

"Is this Dima?"

"Yes, it's Dima," he growls. "Who the fuck are you?"

I push end and snap out the battery. He lowers his phone and jams it in his pocket. I smoke a joint behind the trailer while I wait for him to leave.

Dima leans against the van. Jaw clenched. Brow furrowed. A self-reflective moment I assume is rare. Who could it be? What might they want? Rumination soon gives way to paranoia. He hurries to the hospital door and yanks out the broomstick. Then it's back over to the van to finish packing up. Panicked movements, wild eyes darting from one spot to the next. Like every falling snowflake may pose a unique threat. He slams the back doors shut and throws on his jacket and scrapes the windshield with his sleeve. Then he hops into the van and drives away.

Once he's gone I climb inside the dumpster and retrieve the extra box. It's about the same size as a dresser drawer but nowhere near as heavy as I expected.

Drugs.

Gotta be drugs.

Clear plastic bags stuffed with round red pills. Same as

what I found at Fowst's. Same as what I sold to Angel. And let's be honest, I'll probably sell these too.

I peel off the tape and fold back the flaps and the only thing inside is a bunch of pale green gowns. Hospital scrubs. Like what doctors wear on television.

CHAPTER
THIRTY-ONE

I park in Father's spot behind the church. It's half past two and I'm exhausted. My feet are sore and my socks are wet and my face hurts worse than my feet. I feel like ten tons of shit dumped into a half ton truck. I feel ugly and stupid and weak.

I was never any good at this, despite some good results. Part of it was timing. Part was stubborn pride. Most of it was just brute force. People used to say I was lucky. I always found that funny.

There was nothing lucky or funny about tonight. Tonight was a dead end. Tonight was a hard kick in the balls. And tomorrow I'm back to square one. On top of all that, now I've got competition. I've gotta find Fowst before someone else does.

No need to follow Dima any further. He's no closer to finding Fowst than I am. We've both ignored something, a missing piece that makes the puzzle whole. But if Dima is a dead end, what exactly is the plan?

Good question.

There's only one thing I can do.

Smoke a joint and go to bed.

In the morning I'll hit the spa and check on Mandy. Show her Fowst's phone and that weird second number. Talk to the receptionist and check for matches in her client list. Then it's back to the cafe to question Chelsea.

I'll catch her on her break when the others aren't around. She knows something. I could tell by her tone. Sarcasm is a bad camouflage for guilt. Besides, she's not as dumb as her boss. I bet she spends less time on her phone. I bet she's smart enough to know when she's doing something stupid.

I get home and climb the creaky wooden steps in the dark. Lean against the wall. Fumble with my keys. Grab the knob and watch the unlatched door swing inward like a phantom invitation.

I slip my boots off in the hallway and carry them inside. Smell of pot smoke and perfume. Tall leather boots placed neatly on the mat. A familiar sense of inertia, of inevitability.

I tip-toe through the foyer and lean around the corner. There's a stranger hunched over one of my boxes, rifling through my stuff. Lit joint glowing red in the shadows.

I hit the lights.

Hera straightens up and turns around.

"Take off your coat, old chap. Stay awhile."

I look down and realize I'm still holding onto my boots, still wearing my toque and parka.

"Hope you're not cross," she says flatly, holding up the joint. "I couldn't find any liquor."

"If you're here for a progress report, I haven't made any yet."

"It's certainly not a social call. Let's have ourselves a chat, shall we?"

We sit together at the kitchen table. I tell her everything that's happened so far. She seems bored by the details. She perks up when I mention Mandy. She glances at my bandages but offers nothing close to sympathy. She doesn't ask about Fowst's whereabouts at all.

"You mentioned you gained access to his flat. I'm curious—did you find anything inside?"

"Like what?"

"Valuable objects. Red flags of any kind?"

"Nothing like that."

"You're absolutely certain?"

"Absolutely."

"Very well then."

"My turn," I tell her. "How long have you been up here?"

"Not long."

"How'd you get inside?"

"The shopkeeper," she smirks. "Down below. Nice girl. Very quaint."

"Zahra. What exactly did you tell her?"

"Nothing really. That we are close associates. That you were expecting me. That sort of thing."

"Great."

"What? She's not your girlfriend, is she?"

I say nothing.

Hera stifles a grin. She reaches out to me with the joint held in her fingers like a peace offering. Playful yet condescending, flirting how some douchebag man would flirt.

But I'm too tired for games. A stalemate is the best move I can muster. I take a long deep haul on the joint. Then I take another.

Hera stands and folds her arms across her chest, smugly scanning my apartment. Boxes in a pile against the wall, yet to be unpacked. Hand washed laundry drying on a yard sale bench press. Vintage books stacked in dusty columns like the ruins of an ancient city.

"So," she says, sounding vaguely disgusted. "Have you just moved in?"

CHAPTER
THIRTY-TWO

Hera holds the joint between her lips. I flick the lighter and she leans toward the flame, breathing deeply and exhaling through her nose, twin white shafts that swirl like ghosts between our faces.

"You know," she says. "There is another reason for my visit."

"You wanted to rifle through my stuff?"

"Good Lord. I wanted something to drink and I couldn't find the liquor. I grew quite bored waiting for you to arrive, that's all. You really should get over it."

"Fine. I believe you. What's the other reason?"

"My associates and I would like to offer you a position."

"I'm not even done with this one yet."

"No, not another contract. This would be full-time. Vacation pay. Health benefits. Legitimate long term employment."

"Doing what exactly?"

"We've been watching you, of course. We're very pleased so far. We think you're someone special. We believe you have unlimited potential. We'd like to help you achieve it. There must be something that you want. A purpose, a goal, some mission unfulfilled?"

She's right. I want to walk into the woods without a compass. I want to sail into the sun. I want to set myself on fire.

"I'm sorry you went to all this trouble," I tell her.

"I beg your pardon?"

"There's no point in earning a salary. Not for me at least."

"Forgive me, but I'm truly confused."

"The second I've got something to lose, someone will take it away."

She laces her fingers in a fist beneath her chin. "Go on. Out with it."

So I tell her about Father. That I used to work for him and why. That I didn't want this job in the first place. That all the money goes to him.

Hera never flinches. At times she nods and lifts her eyebrows, urging me to carry on. At times she moves her mouth in a silent sort of way, mimicking my words as if we're reciting the story together. The second that I'm finished talking, she turns to me and says, "Have you ever heard the story of the Lion and the Gnat?"

"No."

"As the fable goes, there's this magnificent lion, who one day finds himself in the presence of a tiny gnat. The gnat flies around, tickling his nose and buzzing past his ears, causing a general nuisance. Eventually, the lion gets angry, roaring and growling to scare the gnat away. And yet, despite this ferocious performance, the little gnat remains indifferent. The gnat says, 'Do you think that I'm afraid, just because they call you King?' Then she flies over and stings the lion's nose. The lion goes wild with rage, swiping and swatting with his claws. And every time he tries to strike the gnat, he ends up slicing himself instead. Unscathed, the gnat stings the lion again and again. Until finally, exhausted and bleeding from his self-inflicted wounds, the lion is forced to surrender. The gnat flies away in triumph, announcing her great victory to all the other creatures on the savanna. Amid this careless boastful flight, she flies directly into a spider's web. And thus she who has just defeated the King is slowly and painfully consumed by another tiny creature, one who is patient and humble and quiet. One who is never blinded by arrogance."

She hauls on the joint and waits for my response.

"So I'm the gnat in this analogy?"

"I'm afraid you've missed the point. The gnat is an irrelevant pest. It's easy to be brave when one's life is worth so little. As for the lion and the spider, there's nothing to learn from either one of them, both are simply acting in accordance with their nature. Make no mistake, the real hero of the fable is the web."

"How do you figure?"

"Think about it. This amazing substance, nearly invisible, spun out of nothing. And yet, a tool of immense power. Sanctuary, paradise, noose, vault, trap, tomb—the structure is without limitations."

"I see."

"Invisible forces run this world. Webs of laws and money. Loyalties that endure the arc of history, the entropy of language, the arbitrage of politics, untouched by war or famine or even death itself. For the lucky fools who glimpse these machinations, only one question remains worth asking: Will you act, or be acted upon? Are you the lion, the gnat, or the web?"

"So I come and work for you? Trade one master for another?"

"Aren't all masters equal?"

"Aren't all slaves?"

"Clever. But let me ask you one last thing. What if there was someone who could clear your debt? Someone who could truly set you free? Wouldn't that be worth your fealty?"

"Like who? A Goddess?"

She doesn't answer. She just stares. Her grin spreads like a plague across her face. Her strange eyes turn to fire.

She slinks toward the bedroom, trench coat slipping off her shoulders. She disappears around the corner but her voice rings out as though she's standing right beside me.

"Submit yourself to progress. Admit you are a fool. It's not too late to be anointed. It's not too late to be reborn. The only way to touch the absolute is absolute destruction."

TRENCH COAT HANGING on the hook behind the door. Clothing in a pile beside the bed. Light spills in through the bedroom window, bathing her skin in a dusty yellow glow.

The only thing she's wearing is a black choker necklace. Lying on her side, knees bent, one arm held across her breasts. A body posed in the shape of a question mark, firm and young and smooth. How many fillers. How many pills. How many trips to the gym. How many corporations made this body?

I edge closer. Propelled by urges I presumed were dead. The urge to play along. To prompt consent. To risk a memory revised. To pull an errant thread. To unravel someone.

She turns her head away, smirking. Withholding her gaze. I graze my fingers down her thigh. I listen to her breathing. I watch her face for signs. I wonder when she might roll over and just how far she'll spread her legs.

In the past this would not have been a game. There would have been consensus. I would have known exactly what it was. And suddenly my lust collapses, replaced by something unexpected. I look down at Hera's perfect body. And realize I'm bored.

XVII

SUNDAY

THIRTY-THREE

I wake up on the floor. Hera's shape still imprinted on the bed. The smell of her hair and skin still hanging in the small cold room. Oddly quiet for a Sunday morning. Shovels scraping distant driveways. Wind howling up the alley like a dog. Muffled voices drifting over from nearby apartments, the whir of their vacuums and dishwashers. Quiet enough to hear Zahra, awake before dawn, rattling around downstairs. Except she isn't there. And I wonder if that's good or bad.

I tear the blanket off the bed and wear it like a cape around my shoulders. Open up the drapes. Scratch the frost off the glass. The blizzard has arrived, parked above the city, choking us in white. Cars buried. Roads obscured. Footprints dotting sidewalks like clues in unsolved crimes.

I make a pot of coffee. I turn on the radio and turn up the heat. I lean against the kitchen counter, staring dumbly at nothing. Soundtracked by psychedelic rock and the drip and gurgle of the coffeemaker.

Something about my desk doesn't look quite right. The lampshade's oblique posture. The absurd position of the chair. The precise re-randomization of my notebooks and pencils and pens. It all seems too prescribed, an imitation of clutter.

The plank beneath the desk is poking up a little.

Impossible.

I pull out the chair and crawl beneath the desk. Pry up the loose floorboards and toss them aside. Plunge my hand into the gap. Buried to my shoulder, fingers brushing spiderwebs and mouse infested insulation, feeling blindly for that polished metal frame. But I come up empty handed. The laptop is gone. The hard drive and the tablet too.

My stomach heaves. I hurry to the closet and rip my parka off the hanger. I turn it upside down and shake it. Nothing falls out.

How long had she been up here, snooping around? Minutes, hours, the whole fucking day?

No Hera.

No laptop.

No key.

But I know exactly where to find them.

CHAPTER THIRTY-FOUR

There's a private city underground. Corporate tunnels built for moving money. Thirty kilometres, twelve hundred stores, the stadium, the aquarium. The Tower.

If you walk around long enough the shops start repeating. Shops that build teddy bears. Shops that sell back rubs. Shops that pluck your eyebrows and wax your pubes. Maybe they have multiple locations. Maybe you've been walking in circles.

The elevator doors slide open. A custodian shimmies her cart to make room. I step on board and press the button. She makes no small talk and that's just fine. I watch the numbers change. I read the newsfeed on the screen above the doors. I picture Hera, sitting alone in a dimly lit office. Black stiletto heels. Tailored pinstriped suit. Swivelled backwards in a leather chair, staring out the window and smoking a cigarette. She spins around to face me. She lifts a little silver gun and points it at my chest.

"Sir? Excuse me sir—it's your floor."

Smart lights wake in sequence as I navigate the hallways. A building full of lawyers is a place I normally avoid, but the storm has kept them all at home. It's just me and the cleaners and this shitty instrumental music. And if I'm lucky, an office door with a lock that's weaker than my foot.

The girl behind the desk doesn't notice me at first. Big brown eyes. Big white teeth. Big round breasts beneath a dark blue blazer. I tap my finger on the glass. She looks up from her computer screen and waves me inside.

"I'll be with you in a moment sir."

I look around the room and wait. Sleek modern decor. Juice bar. Booze bar. Leather couches and a pool table. Meeting rooms and prayer rooms and tiny office cubicles. The view from the conference room is like a sketch in charcoal. Slivers of the lake in the gaps between the towers, island airport runways blinking red inside the storm. A logo on the wall reads, We Are Vertical Solutions.

"Sorry about that. How can I help you today?"

"I might be in the wrong place, but I'm looking for Freedom Capital."

She punches the keyboard. "And I'm checking on that name for you now sir."

"I don't get it."

"So in addition to our co-working spaces we host what's called a virtual office," she says, pointing to the grid of mailboxes on the wall behind her. "So that means we provide a number of business services on behalf of our residential corporate clients."

"Meaning—no one's actually here?"

"Depends on the business. Depends on the day. So I've searched the whole directory and unfortunately I don't see any reservations for that particular client."

"No problem," I tell her, heading for the door. "Sorry to bother you."

Coming here was a stupid idea. I should have got up early. I should have stuck with my original plan.

"Hang on sir," she says, jogging through the lobby in her heels. "Someone left this for you, early this morning. I'm very sorry. I didn't make the connection at first."

We lock eyes as she hands me the package.

"Hope you've got a tux."

ANOTHER ENVELOPE. Waxy black paper. Ink infused with gold. Thinner than the last time. Too thin to be money. An apology? An explanation? Maybe I've been fired. But Hera doesn't make apologies. And our deal's about to expire.

I tear it open and a long stiff card slides out into my palm. Back side completely blank. Three short lines stamped across the front in gold. Address. Time. Dress Code.

I don't attend many parties. Don't often rub shoulders with wealth. I no longer speak the language. I've been exiled from their world.

Maybe it's all just a game. Maybe it's a trap or something worse. But none of that matters. I'll be there regardless. My feet feel light and foolish. My mind rambles like a dog. I'm addicted to inertia. I can't resist what's next.

The arrow turns green. The doors chime and slide apart. A man inside the elevator glances up from his smartphone.

"Going down?"

B y the time the taxi drops me off it's almost dark. I use the super's key and slip inside. Glide across the lobby. Tiptoe past the office. Duck into the stairwell at the far end of the hall. Cinderblock walls. Peeling yellow paint. Footsteps pounding like a hammer as I climb.

I pull my hood down to hide my face, treading softly on the carpet till I get to Fowst's front door. Lock smashed. Doorjamb split like kindling. Door hanging crooked on its hinges.

I step inside. The lights are off and the blinds are shut and there's a dim white light coming from the kitchen. I hold my breath and listen. Someone else is here.

I open the front hall closet and grab a golf club. Press my back against the wall and inch toward the kitchen, heart pounding harder and faster, noises getting louder and stranger. Tin foil crinkle. Hollow metal clank. Wheezing and moaning and now and then a shrill mammalian squeal. And suddenly I feel afraid. Who's behind the wall? Who of us has less to lose?

I burst around the corner. There's two black rats

devouring a rotisserie chicken in the middle of the kitchen floor.

I bring the club down hard. The chicken explodes in loose wet chunks. The smaller rat darts off into the shadows. The big one doesn't move at all. Staring up at me, slick with filth. Beady eyes glowing red in the light from the fridge.

I take another swing but the rat steps sideways, easily dodging the blow. It breaks into a sprint and leaps onto my jeans. Teeth bared, crawling up my thigh toward my crotch. I scream and slap it to the floor. It lands flat on its back, snarling and snapping its jaws. I lift my boot and stomp. Warm guts shoot across the tile in a bright pink rat shaped tube.

I drop the club and hit the lights. The kitchen's been trashed. Fridge and freezer emptied. Drawers and cupboards dumped. Rotten food scattered in a big gross pile across the floor. Routine smash and grab? Too thorough. Teenage vandals? Not thorough enough. No, this is definitely a search. Something small and valuable. Something worth the risk.

I lean against the wall and catch my breath. Scrape the rat juice off my boot sole with a butterknife. The noises start again behind me, louder and wetter than before. I grab the club and turn around.

Half a dozen rats are feasting on the flattened corpse. Squirming bodies packed together, ripping and tearing like an orgy of cannibals.

IT'S the same story in the living room. Bookcase tipped over. Couch cushions slashed. Flatscreen bracket hanging naked on the wall.

The potted plant is not so potted anymore. They ripped

out the tree and dumped out the soil and took the remaining pills.

There's a cheap cellphone on the coffee table with a glass crack pipe and a baggie full of rocks. A sloppy frame job, but maybe just enough to bait a lazy cop. No need to check for prints. I'm sure they'll only find one set.

In the bedroom there's a body. Face down on the carpet, halfway to the bathroom door. The lights are off. The switch is on the other wall. I nudge it with my foot. Nothing happens. I find the lights and hit the switch.

Worn brass lighter still clutched inside his fist. Throat cut ear to ear. Blood pooled on the carpet drying sticky inky black. For a corpse, Pip really gets around.

I bend down and pry the lighter from his stiff little fingers. You can't smoke if you're dead.

Enough sleuthing.

Time to go.

I wipe my prints off the doorknobs and the golf club in the kitchen. I grab the tuxedo and some black leather shoes. I take one last look around.

The man in the painting smiles back thinly, still untouched inside his cheap plastic frame. Wouldn't look too bad on my bedroom wall at home. Maybe Father wants it. Maybe I can sell it.

I grab the sides to lift it off the hook, but the picture frame won't budge. I turn the lights back on and take a closer look. The frame's been painted to the wall, with a bead of caulking smoothed around the edges.

I step over the rats and find a steak knife in the kitchen. Hold it like an ice pick. Drag it down the seams. Every time I accidentally strike the frame, it echoes like an empty drum.

I wipe the knife and drop it on the floor. I take a wad of stuffing from the couch and bundle it around my hand. Then I smash my cushioned fist into the painting. Brush away the broken glass. Tear the shredded poster from the frame. The plastic backing cracks and falls, revealing a compact metal safe mounted crudely in the wall.

Smooth steel finish. Backlit digital display. Bright orange price tag still stuck to the screen, on sale for only five-hundred dollars. I grab the edges, pushing and pulling, trying to work it loose. Two-hundred pounds my ass. Fucking thing weighs a ton.

I try and figure out the code. Punch in random numbers till they fill the tiny screen. Useless. Too many options with an eight digit code. Eight digits...

I type the bogus number from the burner phone. The display turns green. There's a long loud beep and a sharp double click and then the little metal door pops open. The upper shelf holds an envelope stuffed with well-worn fifties and twenties. The bottom shelf holds something else.

I reach inside to pick it up. But I already know what it is. I loosen the string and open the bag and pull out a golden key.

CHAPTER THIRTY-SIX

"Sweet tux. Very dapper. Looks a little tight in the armpits though dude."

"Thank you. It's been quite a while since I've dressed up."

"Same here," Zahra says, rubbing her neck.

I show her the rest of Hera's money. "Can you add this to what's already in the safe? If you don't see me in the next few days, keep half and donate what's left to St. Casimir's."

There's an awkward silence. She folds her arms and hugs her sides. She won't answer me or look me in the eye. "You know that you don't have to go, right?"

"I really do though."

"No, you really don't. You're doing fine. Two jobs, a roof above your head, this big-ass pile of cash. You're doing just fine."

"I know all that. But it's not enough."

"Not enough for what? What more do you want?"

"There's a debt I need to pay."

"Get an extension. Get another loan. Work some overtime. Like any normal person."

"I'm not a normal person. And it's not that kind of debt."

"Honestly dude," she rolls her eyes. "Fuck you and your debt."

Poor Zahra. She thinks she knows me. She thinks she cares. I wish I met her in a different time and place, ten years earlier, twenty years into the future. Less damaged. Less entangled. Better versions of our present selves. But we are the victims of our own decisions. And sliding in is always easier than crawling out.

"The only thing I own is my debt. It's all I think about. It's all I am."

She rushes over and gets right up in my face. "I know her, okay?"

"You know who?"

"That woman," she sighs. "From last night. I know her and I'm telling you, I'm begging you, please don't go."

The telephone rings. Zahra walks back into the shop. I watch her from the doorway. Thin arms trembling. Colour slowly draining from her face. "Okay," she says, before hanging up. Then she flattens her palms on the countertop and starts to cry.

"Who was that?"

"Nobody," she says, wiping her eyes. "Look, I changed my mind. I can totally put that stuff in the safe for you. It's really no problem." She walks me out into the shop and we just stand there, looking at each other, for what seems like a very long time. She checks her watch. "I guess you've got somewhere else to be."

"I guess I do."

And as I walk toward the taxi, I can hear her, behind the door. Bolting every lock.

CHAPTER
THIRTY-SEVEN

The Bridle Path. A gated community without gates. The only gate that matters is the birth canal. The cab drops me off at Park Lane and Post. It's still snowing. The road is one big drift. The wind is cold and hard and dumb. I head south along the curb, scanning driveways for the address on the invitation. I spot some action a few houses down. Luxury cars parked along the shoulder. Little men in matching coats going car to car with flashlights.

Fifth mansion on the left. Concrete wall a few metres off the road. Security guards dressed head to toe in black, holding walkie-talkies, waving cars through heavy iron gates. I smooth my tux and straighten my tie and stride toward the gatehouse.

A guard shines a flashlight in my face. I can tell he thinks it's weird that I'm on foot. I hand him the invitation. He looks me up and down. I fake a shiver and rub my hands together.

"My driver took me to the wrong house."

He buys it.

"Right this way sir."

Long stone walkway winding off into the dark. Construction gear abandoned on the path. Scrap lumber, interlocking brick, a bright blue portable toilet. A plastic sign held in place by sandbags with an arrow pointing east says, Contractor's Entrance.

The walkway leads to a landscaped area enclosed by cedar hedges. Flower beds, shrubs, park benches, a gazebo. Old fashioned lampposts cast pale yellow circles on the freshly shovelled stone.

I exit through a gate in the hedge. Up a slight incline. Onto a well-lit courtyard plaza packed with throngs of people. Ice sculptures, fire-eaters, contortionists. Speakers pumping festive music. Champagne flutes on gleaming silver trays. A private winter party for the city's super rich elites.

The house itself is another story. Mansion is the wrong word. The place looks more like Union Station. It's the kind of spot with an indoor pool and a panic room and a staff that lives on site.

I join a group of guests moving through the crowd toward the house. We slow down to admire a pair of statues at the foot of the steps. Twin sphinxes hewn from solid marble, jet black on the left side, pure white on the right.

A butler greets us in the foyer. Pointing out design features. Directing traffic and collecting coats. White lime-stone floor with beveled marble inserts. Mirrored ceiling faced with antique hand-laid glass. Art deco chandelier, spiky bronze pendants shooting from its centre like a bursting star. What kind of dreams live here. What's left to dream about once your whole life is a dream?

The butler leads us to a vast empty room with vaulted ceilings and a half constructed fireplace roped off with yellow caution tape. There's a makeshift bar staffed by three young women. The lighting is bad. The walls are bare. The floor is caked in dust.

I head directly to the bar. Ambient music plays thinly from a small portable speaker. The guests converse in cold hushed tones. Middle-aged crowd, mostly men and mostly white. None of them look at me. None of them are dressed in formal clothing.

I order a whiskey on ice. I take a drink and look around. There's something gross about these people. I can smell their urges, their sinister anticipation. And another scent, wafting in and out. Musty with a tinge of sulphur.

"Hey man," says one of the bartenders. It's Chelsea, from the cafe, all dolled up in a slim black dress. "You should totally not be here right now."

"I'm guessing neither should you."

"Look," she whispers, leaning closer. "I'm not sure what your whole deal is, or whatever, but I'm honestly trying to help you. Trust me. You need to get the frig out of this place. Like turn around and go."

The butler sidles up next to us, grinning like a smug little fuck. "May I see your ticket sir?"

"My ticket?"

"Yes. Your ticket. Little black and gold card. Wallet sized."

I pull it out and hand it over.

He takes a look and gasps.

"You're supposed to be in the auditorium," he says, snatching the drink from my hand. "And the bar is for guests only."

I look around for Chelsea but she's vanished.

"Come on, hurry up!"

He leads me down a long dirty corridor strung with temporary lighting. We exit through a steel door and end up in a small round foyer with a checkerboard pattern on the floor.

"The auditorium is right through there," he says, pointing at the double doors to our right. "The Inner Order is already seated. You are to help the Outer Order to their seats. You are to treat their guests as you would treat a full-fledged member. Once the Doctor takes the stage, you are to remain on call until the lecture concludes. Is that clear?"

I nod once and say nothing. He sighs and shows me to the door. I take a quick look back as I enter the auditorium. Our tuxedos match.

THIRTY-EIGHT

"So I thought we could begin with the intersectionality of existential philosophy and physical posture..."

The auditorium looks more like a gymnasium. A basketball court constructed by a rich imposter. Temporary stage, rented lights and curtains, pompous wizened man behind the lectern with a voice like a wild west prospector.

"...you know, the real question is, what traits make lobsters so damn successful in their undersea societies?"

Dust hangs in the glare of the lights. The air smells like glue and varnish. I press my back against the wall and scan the crowd for Hera. Thirty rows of folding chairs. One hundred wealthy patrons, faces split in half by light and darkness.

"...and never mind these eighteenth century Marxists and their useless critiques of modern capitalism. It's just never been true. Not even a little bit..."

He speaks of animal hierarchies and managed meritocracies, of heroic male figures in greek mythology and professional sport, of decadence and nihilism, of destruction and renewal. Baby-boomer grievance masquerading as objective truth. Pseudo-scientific nonsense, amplified by algorithms, monetizing a single insidious message: this is the world and it will never change.

And yet the crowd remains transfixed. And I wonder if I've missed something, if we're hearing the same thing.

"When I walk down the street, I can distinguish, on sight, the kids that wrestle their fathers from the ones who don't. It's just really important. Kids love to wrestle their fathers. It's really good for them. Kids who don't wrestle their fathers are chubby and awkward and other kids don't want to play with them."

I cringe and turn toward the audience, expecting laughter. But something different happens. Eyes sparkle, cheeks flush, clever grins emerge. And then I get it. The man himself is unimportant. The man is a disposable rube. They only want him for his platform. The votes those clicks will generate. The profits that will follow.

"...and in conclusion, even among chimpanzees, it's not a good idea to be a tyrant. Thanks everybody. Have a great night."

The Politician lumbers up the steps and heaves himself across the stage. "My friends, let's have a big round of applause for our very special guest, Doctor Patterson."

The men shake hands and pose for photos. The house lights come up slowly. The butler makes announcements on the mic.

"All members of the Inner Order may proceed to the lounge. Directions have been marked out on the floor with bright green tape. Please ensure your talisman is visible. Members of the Outer Order and their distinguished guests are free to congregate in the Great Room. Refreshments will be served. The ascension ceremony will begin at nine o'clock."

The crowd shuffles to the exit. But one guest doesn't

move at all. Black bowler hat. Bleached white face. Sunken rings around his eyes. Standing dead still in the back row, watching me.

I elbow through the exit line, heading for the stage. Annoyed grumbling, smell of aftershave and dry-cleaned clothes. I trip over an extension cord. The stage lights flicker. I get back on my feet and break into a run. Dress shoes squeaking on the hardwood. Thin man plowing through the folding chairs behind me.

I trace the cord to a plug behind the stage. The thin man rounds the corner, lanky shadow stretched like fingers on the floor. I rip out the plug. The lights go off. Puzzled patrons murmur in the exit line as the last few guests trickle out the door.

Pitch black now. Just me and the thin man and the dark. I slide along the wall searching for a window or a door. My fingers graze a doorframe. I turn the doorknob but it's locked. I shuffle down a little further. Fire extinguisher. Thermostat. Another locked door.

The wall changes texture. I slip my palms from left to right, heartbeat drowning out my breath, feeling my way forward like a mime. The thin man's back there, inching closer. I can taste him and smell him. I can hear him breathing through his teeth.

I take another careful step. A piece of flooring clicks beneath my heel. The whole wall vibrates. Then it spins in place like a carnival ride.

CHAPTER
THIRTY-NINE

I end up in a closet. For a secret room, it's nothing special. Breaker panels. Server cabinet. Fibre optic cables strung in bright blue plastic bundles. I stick my head into the corridor.

Construction seems finished in this wing of the house. Plush silk carpets. Architectural lighting. Equidistant doors repeating like a luxury hotel.

Dance music thumps in the distance. The bass seeps up into my feet. The air is thick and damp and tastes like pomegranate. I take off my jacket and hang it on the doorknob. Unclip my tie and drop it on the floor. I unbutton my collar and roll up my sleeves and follow the beat down the hall.

Vaulted double doors behind a classy velvet rope. A bouncer blocks the entrance. Shaved head. Neck tattoo. Thick arms folded on a broad barrel chest.

"Your talisman sir?"

"Sorry what?"

"Need to see your talisman."

I take out the key and hold it up. His eyes widen for a moment, then his face turns back to stone.

"Go ahead sir."

I wade into a moist cavernous room. Two levels. Three bars. Strobe lights and lasers and a mirrorball. Smoke machine fog drifts through the crush of bodies writhing on the dance floor, coloured tiles flashing on and off beneath their feet. The song concludes and in the lull before the next one starts, I hear a woman's worn out voice, moaning desperately.

I climb the steps to the mezzanine and grab two drinks from the upstairs bar. I lean against the railing, drinking quickly and scanning the crowd. Dank pit packed with dancers. Naive young women in heels and skirts. Greasy predatory men. Like any club in any town, except here they all wear masks, like some kind of masquerade ball. Who are these people. How many were present at the lecture. How many are members. How many are guests?

The music shifts to something slow and lurching. The lights become subdued, synchronizing with the playlist. I spot a glass door across the mezzanine, vaguely human shapes in motion behind the frosted pane of glass. I slide along the railing, feeling good. Feeling right at home in the seedy darkness of the little upstairs bar.

The mystery door leads to an ornate lounge. Barman mixing drinks. Private u-shaped booths faced in walnut or mahogany. Women circled on a compact dance floor, arms raised, swaying in placid unison. Maniac smiles amplified by the strangeness of their masks.

I move from booth to booth, peering through the gaps in the drapes. People fighting. People fucking. People nodding off against the cushions, eyes drooped, faces twitching. One of the dancers spots me. She breaks away from the group, sauntering over like she's in some sort of trance. Black and gold venetian mask. Long black gown like the one at Mandy's condo. She reaches out and takes my hand.

"Are you a stranger?"

"I'm nobody."

"You must be here for a reason. Are you an initiate? A proxy? Maybe just a fool?"

"I'm here to finish a job."

The woman smiles. She rests my hand on the small of her back, laughing as we move to the beat, steering my hips with her own. Smooth amber skin. Thick braided hair. Eyes like twin black coals. And every time I think that I know her, I realize I don't. She's an amalgam. A composite. She's someone you encounter in a dream.

"How dare you trespass here without your mask? How dare you interrupt these rites?"

"I didn't have a choice."

"Choice is an illusion," she whispers as we glide toward the others. She leans in closer. Her cheek softly grazes my chin. She slides her hand across my stomach and rests it on my hip, grinding her pelvis up and down my thigh. She lowers my fly and slides her hand into my pants. "I know the reason you are here. You are here to be reborn."

I flinch and pull away.

Restore the empty space between our bodies.

"Acquiesce," she says, arm extended, hand still buried in my trousers. The dancers encircle us, bobbing and lurching and tearing off their clothes. She wraps her fist around my dick, pulling until we're pressed together once again. Staring from behind her mask. Panting on my neck and chest. "Acquiesce. Destroy yourself completely. You won't be safe until you do."

I nod yes and we begin to twirl. Slowly at first, then faster and faster, till the other faces melt together like a strange collage, friends and family, random people on the street, every face I've ever seen that's ever lived and breathed and died. The music gets louder. The dancers tighten their circle, eyes blank, limbs flailing. Her grip loosens. Her hand pumps harder and faster. The tempo surges. The dancers cave inward. She jerks and pulls and squeezes. Salty fingers shove pills into my mouth as I cum into her hand. The dancers overwhelm us and I'm swallowed by the mob, mindless animals, fed by noise and chaos.

Time slows. My vision blurs. My feet won't touch the floor. The woman is a captured fly, cocooned in other people's limbs. Our eyes meet. Her mouth gapes. Her voice is soundless and horrible. I tear myself away, falling through the twisting bodies till I'm laying on the floor.

Eventually the music stops. The sound of footsteps fades. I stand and zip my pants and pour myself a drink behind the bar. The dancers have all vanished. The people in the booths as well. My pockets have been emptied. The golden key is gone. The moaning noise is back again, closer and louder than before.

I follow the sound down a long empty corridor. I feel nauseous and my clothes are drenched in sweat.

I walk until I reach a pleated set of drapes. Thick red velvet, floor to ceiling like a wall. I brush my hand along the folds until I find a seam and slip inside.

Single spotlight on the ceiling. Zigzag patterns on the floor. A dozen people grouped around a wooden table, chanting softly. Faces hidden under long black hooded robes.

A muffled voice cries out. The air smells sick and sweet. There's a naked woman tied spread-eagled on the table, eyes bulging, mouth taped shut. Muscled body writhing as the laser cuts incisions on her hip.

They turn off the machine and douse the wound with fluid. The woman screams into the duct tape, bucking hard at her restraints. They remove the swab and undo the straps and reveal the putrid brand:

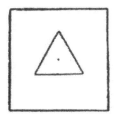

Skylar sits up on her elbows, nude and beaming. She tucks her legs beneath her hips and stands up proudly on the table, joining in with the others as the chant grows louder and louder. Only then do I understand the words.

"...this is the way the world is...this is the way the world is...this is the way the world is...this is the way the world is..."

CHAPTER FORTY

I slink away and duck beneath the drapes. Moving quickly, trying not to think, rambling through an unfinished wing of the enormous house. Stud walls. Sawdust on the concrete floor. Sheets of thick grey plastic stapled over window frames.

I walk for what seems like a long time. Until the hallway ends. There's an empty doorway and a staircase going down. Bare wood steps. No railings. No lights. It's either down, or back the way I came.

I descend slowly. Feeling sick and getting worse. Pitch black at the bottom, damp and cold like a basement. I should have counted my steps. I should have tied a string.

Structures taking shape before me. Smell of chlorine or ammonia or bleach. Hushed voices. Gentle music. A steady electronic beep. Plain white bedsheets tacked to the rafters. Shadows moving on the other side.

The bedsheets form a wall across the basement. I find a flap and crawl inside. The room is set up like a luxurious military hospital. Persian rugs, hardwood tables, diagnostic gear and other medical devices. Two gurneys set up side by side like twins.

On the left there's an elderly man, fast asleep. Sleeve rolled up. Necktie loosened. Dinner jacket folded neatly on the railing of the bed. A thin red tube stuck into his forearm connects to a blood bag hanging from a silver pole. I trace my eyes along the tube, across the gap between the beds, into the thin pale arm of the young girl on the gurney next to him. Bare legs sticking out beneath her gown. Toes curled inside her soiled white socks.

I clench my fists and make my way toward them. The old man stirs and sees me coming. His eyes bulge. He opens up his mouth to shout. I punch him in the face until he passes out.

The girl opens her eyes. It's the green-haired chick from the shelter system. Sleeping rough one night, selling blood the next. I wonder how she got here and how much fucked up shit they made her do. What happened to her parents? Is she an orphan too? I reach out and grab the tube.

"Let's get you out of here."

"Wait," she says, shoving me away. "What the hell are you doing?"

"Rescuing you. Stop making it so difficult."

"No way I'm leaving till I get paid."

"You can't just sit here and let them do this. I won't let you."

"Oh I get it," she says, rolling her eyes. "You think you're a superhero or something. Big tough man flying in to save the day. Come on. Get a life. It's my body and it's my choice and it's easy money. End of story. Go away."

I'm about to tell her there's more important things in life than money, but the words sound false inside my head. Like a controlling Dad warning his kid about marijuana while he pours himself another drink.

The girl's eyes dart sideways. I turn around as a nurse

stabs me in the stomach. I hit her once in the face and she drops like a pale green sack.

"Holy shit. Are you okay?"

I look down and there's a scalpel protruding from my side, flat steel blade buried to the hilt. "I don't feel anything yet."

"You better go," she says with sudden kindness. "There's dozens of us down here. The medics will come after you. And worse people too."

I stumble down the middle of the makeshift rooms. More nurses, more gurneys, more blood bags for the rich. People from my neighbourhood. Strangers with faces that I recognize. Hospital waiting rooms. Bus shelter benches. Dollar store checkout lines.

I plow into the final room and rip down all the sheets and finally I'm alone again in the dark. Wandering through empty space, without purpose or direction, without the slightest notion of the ceiling or the walls. But I keep it moving. Away from the clinic. Toward an exit or a resolution. Toward some kind of end. Every few steps a sting of pain flares up my side. The knife.

Leave it in, or pull it out?

I pull it out. The pain drops me to my knees. Blood pours down my stomach, collecting in a warm wet pool around my crotch. And this is where they'll find me. In the hole again. Bled out in a basement in a filthy borrowed tux.

I collapse onto the floor and close my eyes. I lay there for a long time. I think about entropy. I think about debt. I think about destiny and choices, existence and reality. Violence is what matters. Pain is the only thing that's real.

I see my life expressed as a statistic, a single line of text in someone's annual report, stuffed inside a manilla folder, delivered to a bureaucrat preoccupied with lunch.

I think about Father.

I think about Zahra and Mandy and Hera.

Most of all, I think about freedom.

RUSTLING IN THE SHADOWS. Blunt snout sniffing like a dog. The dead raccoon stumbles into view. Walking upright on its hind legs, one paw holding in its guts.

"Come on bud," it says. "Don't give up quite yet."

I get up on my hands and knees. The raccoon leads the way and we plod on together through the dark. Clinic lighting dwindling behind us. Total blackness like a cave.

The raccoon walks with a limp, favouring its wounded side. The blood dripping from my stomach makes tiny splashes on the floor.

The raccoon hums a tune and snaps its raccoon fingers. Eventually, I start humming too.

Lights flicker faintly up ahead. The raccoon looks at me and winks. "Almost there bud."

Bodies moving strangely in the torchlight. Odours I don't recognize. People speaking in tongues. Camping lanterns set on wooden stools. We pass by two dead pigs splayed out like gutted husks. Throats carved open, fresh blood flowing into drains in the floor.

There's a tangled mass of greasy limbs squirming in the centre of the room. Thrusting buttocks, scissoring hips, bare skin stained in blood. Men? Women? I can't be certain. All I see are selfsame faces, moaning in empty pleasure. Dominated by imitation and envy and ritual.

We squeeze between the twitching bodies. Some of them hiss like cats. Others block our path, molesting us with probing bloodstained fingers.

Finally we vacate the orgy. The exit is another wall of

drapes. I take another step, wanting to go forward. But the dead raccoon won't budge.

"Don't look behind the curtain," it says.

"Why not?"

"He who seeks the Goddess seeks the end."

CHAPTER FORTY-ONE

The raccoon disappears. Drumbeats lure me through the drapes. A single lamp provides the only light. A ring of naked drummers pound skin drums in a steady driving rhythm. Within the circle, barely visible in the flickering darkness, are three silhouettes. Only two of them look human.

I move toward the drummers, peering through their limbs. Something's squatted on a heavy iron box. A giant creature with the body of a man, but the head of a bull or a goat.

Matted black fur. Curled onyx horns gleaming silver in the lamplight. Snorting and stomping its heels to the rhythm. Iron chains stretch from the box to the shackled necks of two nude slaves, one male and one female.

The beast reaches down and rattles the chains. The slaves crawl forward. The drumming gets louder and faster. The beast tears off its loincloth and thrusts out its hips. Loose pectorals resting on a pale ribcage. Pot belly quivering with every wheezing breath.

The slaves lean in. Both their heads start bobbing up and down. The pace quickens. The beast lets out a high pitched squeal. The woman stops and pulls away. She wipes her mouth across her arm and bursts into tears. Dark brown tan. Big pale breasts. Blonde hair pulled back into a ponytail.

The man slides sideways on his knees, hands and forearms covered in tattoos, scrotum swinging loose between his thighs. He reaches out and rubs the woman's shoulders.

"It's okay Mandy," Dima whispers. "Everything is okay."

The beast stomps loudly on the box. The drumming stops. Mandy sobs and sobs, face pushed into Dima's tattooed chest. I look up from the slaves and lock eyes with the beast. Milky yellow pools confined to ugly puckered craters, coaxing me into submission.

His gaze assumes control. I can't speak or move or look away. Frozen in both time and space, watching from outside my body. The beast lifts its arm and slowly curls its index finger.

"Come here," it says.

My legs obey, carrying me closer. Just a few more steps until I'm there. Mandy screams. Her voice breaks the trance. I grab the lamp and hurl it at the beast. The glass shatters and the box bursts into flames. The beast shrieks, leaping up and down inside the blaze. Burning kerosene races across the floor and ignites the heavy drapes and within seconds the room is an inferno.

The drummers flee toward the exit. Dima, still shackled to the box, flails like a madman in the shimmering heat. Mandy sits on the floor and wails, reaching for me through the fire.

I dart back to the orgy room, shouting for help. Searching for a blanket or a fire alarm or a tap with running water. Through the smoke I see the woman from the lounge, dodging fleeing hedonists, treading lightly through the puddled blood. She finds a seam in the drapes and spreads them apart, revealing a narrow doorway in the concrete basement wall. She looks around for a moment. Then she disappears inside.

I hear a dull wet thud behind me. And then another and another. I turn around, walking backwards, watching Mandy smash her face against the floor until she's swallowed by the flames.

CHAPTER
FORTY-TWO

The staircase spirals upwards through the innards of the house. The woman's footsteps echo above me. I follow the sound through the dark. She leads me to a long bright hallway. No smoke alarms, no sirens. No sign of any fire.

A threshold appears from nothing in the distance. Ornate doors swing open, revealing a dimensionless space, lit by the whiteness of the floor. On a raised platform in the room's centre there's a woman seated on an antique silver throne. Globed crown atop her head. Gold mask hiding most of her face. Lavish flowered veil hovering behind her like a wall.

The woman from the lounge is on her knees before the throne. Head bowed. Small black bag in her palms like a sacred offering.

"Who dares to penetrate the outer temple?" the crowned woman says, thick red lips barely moving as she speaks, white robe shimmering like a galaxy of stars.

"I do, Priestess."

"Stand up and remove your mask."

The woman nods once and obeys. She takes off her

mask. A scar wraps around her neck like a soft purple ribbon. I still can't see her face.

"Have you studied the ancient texts?"

"Yes, Priestess."

"Do you understand the symbols?"

"Yes, Priestess."

"Did you acquire the sacred keys?"

"Yes, Priestess

"Bring them to me."

She loosens the bag and removes the keys and gently hands them over. Behind her mask, the Priestess's eyes assume a sinister glow. "Congratulations, Initiate. You may enter the Inner Temple."

The woman bows and disappears behind the veil. I take a long deep breath and make my way toward the throne, limping heavily, favouring my wounded side. Blood trickles down my leg and leaves a trail of droplets on the floor. I'm sick and dizzy and seeing coloured spots, floating rainbow blobs that burst and morph and shimmer.

The Priestess hears me coming. She puts the keys aside and points her mask in my direction, cruel eyes lingering on my wounds. "Proxies are not permitted in the temple. You must leave here at once."

"Too bad I'm not a proxy."

"I beg your pardon, fool?"

"You heard me. What's behind the wall?"

"The veil hides many secrets."

"I bet. Is she back there or not?"

"Who?"

"The Goddess."

"I cannot say for certain," she smirks. "The Goddess does not present herself to the uninitiated."

"No? What about me?"

She scans my torso, eyes the warm red stain spreading up

my shirt, the inky blood spilling from my shoe. "You seek a cure? For your ailments?"

"I guess you could say that."

"You've read the sacred texts? You understand the ancient symbols?"

"I've done none of those things."

"Then you have your answer, don't you fool?"

I shrug my shoulders and drag myself toward the veil. The Priestess leaps to her feet, bellowing archaic incantations, gesticulating madly with her arms. She jumps on my back and sinks her teeth into my neck. I knock the crown off her head and grab a handful of hair and rip out a greasy clump. She screams through her teeth and clamps down harder. Warm blood squirts between her lips, streaming down my neck and chest.

I lurch toward the throne. Priestess still glued to my back, bony legs clamped tight around my waist. I snatch a key and tilt my head and shove it hard over my shoulder.

It goes in deep at first. But I push it in a little further. Until it's easy. Until my fist feels warm and wet.

Her jaw relaxes. Her body goes completely limp. She slides down my back and hits the floor. Golden key half-buried in the dewy red hole where her eyeball used to be.

I kick her in the ribs.

I wait until I'm sure she's dead.

I rip the sleeve off my shirt and wipe the blood off my neck. Then I take the other key and lift the flowered veil and step inside the temple of The Goddess.

CHAPTER FORTY-THREE

T he space beyond the veil is a perfect mirror of the outer temple, identical in every way but one. Instead of a throne it holds a glowing globe-shaped monolith. Colours swirl like colliding storms across its glossy surface. Millions of tiny pictures, appearing and dissolving on its curving screen-like shell. And the longer I look at it, the bigger it gets.

A lonely voice cries out. Howling in disenfranchised fury. One voice becomes a thousand. Millions become billions. Two billion banshee voices, everywhere and nowhere, shrieking all at once. At first the noise is deafening. But I grow accustomed to it quickly. I'm so mesmerized by the monolith, I don't care about anything else.

I reach out and touch it with my fingers and my hand slides right inside. Laminated in the flow, like touching a waterfall. I push my arm in further. And then my chest and shoulders. I keep pushing till I'm totally absorbed.

Shrieking voices muted. Kaleidoscope walls shimmering with liquid crystal light. Boundaries collapse. Public and private coalesce. My interior world crumbles and slips away.

A cradle appears before me, rocking gently in the ether.

I inch closer and peer down upon a little baby girl, sound asleep on a mattress made of peacock feathers. I watch her sleeping for a moment. Wonder who created her and why. Who left her here, developing in isolation, without rules or supervision?

Her eyelids flicker open. She furrows her brow. Her chest stops moving. Her face turns crimson red. She's choking.

I pry open her jaw. Something's lodged inside her throat. I stick my fingers in her mouth and yank the object loose. She's paralyzed at first, eyes bulging, gagging on a mouthful of air. And then finally she breathes. She moves her little arms and kicks her little legs. Her face relaxes. Her skin regains its normal colour.

The gold coin pinched between my fingers feels heavy and important. The only thing that matters. The only thing that's real.

I glance back down. The baby's face has changed. Her eyes have turned to blanks, lustrous blue orbs, staring back at me, unblinking and horrendous.

I'm about to call for help when she's beset by a series of convulsions. Heavy spasms rack her tiny torso. Her stomach rolls and heaves. She grins up at me in a way that no baby has ever grinned. Then she lifts her legs and shits.

Liquid excrement engulfs the crib, spewing out between the slats, collecting in a noxious golden pool across the bright white glowing floor.

The stench is overwhelming. I back away, nauseous and afraid. My feet slip out from underneath me. I waver for a second, both arms whirling, body floating horizontal in the air. I come down hard, directly on my tailbone. Wounded stomach torn wide open. Clothing drenched in hot gold shit.

"Is this the Goddess?" I shout.

But I already know the answer.

Everybody does.

I get back up on my feet. Treading through the sewage. Both hands holding in my guts. Someone's moving fast behind me, running flat-out in the filth. A blackened fist slams like steel into my face. My front teeth break. My mouth fills up with blood. My legs give out and I splash down into darkness. And the golden waste becomes my world.

CHAPTER FORTY-FOUR

I had a dream. I'm standing on a ledge above a bottomless pit. Pressed against the chasm wall, dirty blistered feet kicking loose stones into space.

The ledge is lined with men. Thousands of them, spiralling up for miles toward a tiny patch of sky. Dour sullen men, around my age and size, trudging up the narrow track, inches from death. Each of them believing they will someday reach the top.

Every few minutes there's another long scream as a body disappears in the abyss. I watch them fall until they vanish but I never hear them hit the ground.

At night the sky rains oil. Heavy brown bitumen, greasing the ledge, staining my feet, mixing with the sweat on my forehead, running down my cheeks like tears.

To pass the time they whisper stories. Gazing up toward the surface, telling tales of a pale grey disc that never seems to get any bigger. Some say it's a lush garden paradise. Others claim it's a portal, a rift in time that takes you to another world—a better one.

I listen to them gossip. They don't realize they've missed the point. The exit shaft only fits one man at a time. I know this. I've known it all along. I know that when I reach the top, I'll have a simple choice to make. Throw somebody down, or be thrown down myself.

But we have weeks and months left to climb. So for now, I'll just keep shuffling along. Calm and patient and polite. Watching other bodies fall.

MONDAY

CHAPTER
FORTY-FIVE

I wake up somewhere dark that smells like piss and puke and shit. The only sound is dripping water, each drop like the ticking of a clock.

"Am I still alive?"

I whisper this out loud. But no one else is here. And I'm too cold to be dead. I roll over and rest my head against the ground and soon I'm floating just above the cold steel floor, electric skin blurring at the edges, waves of sound and colour crashing over me again and again and again.

I PEEL my face off the floor. Head throbbing. Wrists restrained with plastic ties behind my back. Pip's brass lighter is still inside my pocket. I can feel it underneath my thigh. If I can slip my wrists beneath my hips, maybe I can grab it.

I drive my forearms down my back, pushing hard until the plastic breaks the skin. Mouth pouring water. Rank breath hanging thickly in the air.

I turn my head and puke. Hot bile sucks into the empty

holes where my front teeth used to be. And the only thing that happens next is pain.

I give up trying to escape. Exhausted. Shivering in the dirt. Swollen shredded mouth leaking puss and lymph. I listen for a long time. I hear wind and birds and water. I hear cars in the distance, driving fast.

But I've done all this before. I've waited for sounds. Boots on bare concrete. Doors that slam like bombs. Solitary men, boxed and stacked. Howling into drain pipes.

I've listened and I've waited and I've watched. Wild eyes caught behind narrow windows, desperate foreheads pressed against the glass. That depraved silhouette, leering in the doorway, brutal and familiar. Nooses weaved from shredded bedsheets. Swollen toes that don't quite touch the floor. Yellow cinderblock walls, scratched by fingernails and painted over.

Dim shapes emerge around me. Tuxedo pants torn at the knees. Borrowed shoes spattered in someone else's blood. My useless lower body splayed like meat across the floor.

The bar of light beneath the door gets stronger. I get up on my elbow and take a look around. Gas cans stored on a rusty metal rack. Coils of rope and cable. Hand tools cluttered in a battered wooden box, chisels, screwdrivers, tin snips and pliers, a pipe wrench and a ball-peen hammer. And leaning in the corner, blade gleaming faintly in the early morning light—a brand new long handled axe.

A vehicle stops outside the doors. It sounds like a van or a truck. I get my balance and try to climb onto my feet but find my ankles are zip-tied together.

The driver cuts the engine. I roll onto my stomach. Crawling on my elbows like a soldier. Headed for the rack against the wall. His feet hit the ground. He stops and coughs and spits. I spin myself around, upright on my knees, inching backwards, reaching for the toolbox on the shelf. His keyring jingles as he fiddles with the locks. My fingers graze the pliers. The padlock clicks. Chains rattle through the flange. Stubborn hinges squeal as he hauls backward on the doors.

Sunlight brightens the container and for a moment I'm blinded by the glare. I see water stretching south toward America. I see the pure blue azure sky. I see a towering shadow, jet black against the sun. And a heavy boot swinging hard into my face.

CHAPTER FORTY-SIX

F ace down in the dirt again. Waiting for the needle or the knife. His jacket hits the floor. His shirt and sweater too. Rough hands grabbing at my clothing, fumbling near my groin. I kick him in the shins and crawl away on my elbows. Face throbbing. Blood flowing freely down my wrists and forearms.

He unbuckles his belt and drops his trousers. I can hear him panting. I can smell his balls. He steps into the shade and I see him clearly for the first time. Big nose. Beady eyes. Maple leaf tattooed onto his arm. Burn scars seared across his neck and chest. Angry blisters on his shins. The leather man, the crooked cop, the beast. He's all of them. Everywhere. Ubiquitous.

He shoves his crotch into my face and I'm confronted by the horror of his genitalia. Twin white worms, larval and translucent, fully engorged. And dangling underneath, nearly hidden by a nappy thatch of pubes, an enormous distended testicle, veiny and pulsating and blue. He grabs the back of my head, grinning wildly.

"TIME TO EAT IT CUNT."

Church bells echo in the harbour. A thrill passes through me like a shining golden wave.

THE SURGE.

I snap off the restraints and cast them both aside. Then I wrap my fists around his dicks and pull. He screams and tumbles backwards, clutching the gushing red patch between his legs. I fling his torn-off dicks into the snow like I'm feeding pigeons at the mall.

He drags himself into the yard, howling. Desexed groin producing juicy crimson slush. I grab the axe and follow him outside. The ringing in my ears is everything. THE SURGE is my whole world.

I let him crawl across the access road. Box him in until he's up against the fence. He stops and rolls onto his back.

"You know you'll end up back there," he sneers.

"I served my time."

"Every sentence is a life sentence. Haven't got that figured out yet, do ya cunt?"

"I've figured out a lot of things lately. I've seen a few things too. Witnessed them, in fact."

"Yeah? And who the fuck is gonna listen to a shitbird bitch like you? You're not gonna kill me. You're not gonna rat. You're not gonna do a single fucking thing."

I lift the axe onto my shoulder. "No?"

"No," he grins. "Besides, it'd be a real shame if something happened to the kid."

"What the fuck did you just say?"

"You heard me. The kid. At the church."

I say nothing.

"Thought we didn't know? Well, guess what? We do. And what about your pretty flower girl...boy oh boy...she's a tasty little number, ain't she? We know everything there is to know about her. We know her inside and out..."

I lift the axe above my head.

It feels heavy and righteous and good.

It's more about the weight than how hard you swing. But I swing hard anyway, with my whole body. Because I want to. Because I can.

The axe falls again and again. Blunt side down, each blow a little harder than the last. His femurs take some work. His forearms snap like twigs. His neutered cries echo through the Port Lands. And it sounds like freedom.

CHAPTER
FORTY-SEVEN

I grab a table at the deli on the corner of Bathurst and Bloor. I'm too late for lunch and too early for dinner and Hera has yet to arrive. It's warm outside and the sidewalks are jammed with people. Pale and bewildered, soaking up the sun before it goes away. Fat guys with tattooed calves wearing cargo shorts and sandals. Middle-aged women strutting in their running gear, rejuvenated by the miracle of spandex pants.

People crowd along the temporary fence across the street. Gawking at the flat brown delta where the old emporium once stood. The building seemed to vanish overnight. Demolished without a trace. Replaced by signage, mud and water. Seagulls bathing in a dirty shallow pond.

I sip my coffee with the good side of my mouth, thinking back. Free turkeys at Christmas and Thanksgiving. Twenty thousand light bulbs in the sign. The old man in the commercials, his honest voice and face. The kind of store that could only have existed here, on this exact corner, in our modest city of the past.

A billboard bolted to the safety fence says Condos Coming Soon. In the ad, a bare chested boy with curly blonde hair rides bareback on a galloping white horse. He wears a wreath of roses on his head. His long yellow banner ripples in the wind.

Another section has been turned into a mural. Infinite sunflowers stretching back beneath a perfect blue sky. Throngs of people have materialized, posing for photos, as if the flowers are real. Stomachs flexed. Tongues stuck out. Pursed lips and sucked-in cheeks like the ducks in the pond behind the fence.

"You shaved."

"Twenty stitches in my mouth. Didn't have a choice."

Hera folds her coat over her arm and slides into the booth. Thin grey turtleneck. Small gold watch. Hair pulled back in a thick french braid. She opens her purse and pulls out an envelope and pushes it across the table.

"My client is very grateful."

"For what?"

"Your services, of course."

"I can't accept the money."

"And why is that?"

"Because I failed. Never found Fowst. Never even came close. Don't think I did, at least. The advance you paid was generous. Why don't we just leave it at that?"

"I disagree wholeheartedly."

"Okay," I tell her, confused. "Is that all you're going to say?"

"Indeed. Although I suppose a word of thanks would be appropriate. In the past, our other contractors have lacked your...tenacity. You did your utmost to honour the spirit of our agreement and those efforts did not go unnoticed. I trust you'll find the compensation more than satisfactory."

I shrug and put the money in my pocket.

"Also," she says shyly, imitating someone who blushes. "I got you something."

She sets a small gift-wrapped box on the table.

"What is it?"

"You'll see."

I watch her for a long time. Search her face for something real. And then it hits me. There's nothing there to find.

"Thanks," I tell her. "I'll open it later."

"Well," she says, gathering her coat. "I suppose I should be going."

"Hang on a second. I've got something for you too."

She raises an eyebrow.

I slide the golden key across the table.

"I think this belongs to you."

"Keep it," she says, holding back a smile. "I don't need it anymore."

THE FIVE O'CLOCK news comes on the deli television:

"...fire broke out at a North Toronto construction site early Monday morning. Crews worked quickly to extinguish the blaze. No injuries were reported. The nearly completed luxury mansion was almost totally destroyed.

The identities of the owners are still unknown. A statement from police indicates the property is held by a limited liability corporation registered in an offshore jurisdiction. Further complicating the matter is the property's presence on several holiday rental websites.

This incident comes just weeks after the gruesome double murder of a billionaire couple in Toronto's upscale Bridle Path neighbourhood. A full police investigation has now been launched. A Toronto Police spokesperson would not confirm or deny the incidents may be linked..."

. . .

BACK OUTSIDE I take a look at Hera's money. Drag my thumb across the edges, counting quickly, scanning for fakes. Worn out fifties. Pale green twenties. Random purple tens like jokers in a deck of cards.

Someone revs an engine in a parking spot across the road. Bright blue sports car. Tinted windows with a blower on the hood.

Hera comes striding down the sidewalk. Loaded down with shopping bags. Hips swaying like a model. She puts the bags into the trunk and circles to the passenger side. She opens the door. Light pours in. For a moment, I can see inside the car. Broad male shoulders. Short hair neatly combed. Pale pink polo shirt with the collar popped.

I watch the car until it disappears. Hera's gift still clutched inside my hand. I tear off the wrapper and wiggle off the lid. It's a custom set of business cards. Matte black. My real name stamped across the front in gold:

William Keele
Security Consultant
Freedom Capital

The birds on the pond erupt. Beating their wings against the water. Cackling like fools.

I toss the cards into the trash can. I don't want the job, no matter what it pays. But I'm keeping the name.

The sun emerges from behind a cloud, bathing the street in warm golden light. The past comes rushing back to me. And I remember.

The Island. The Market. The Exhibition. The smell inside my grandfather's apartment. The playground in the park behind our house. Sitting with my buddies on the school bus, the way we lived to make each other laugh. The life and heart and mind the city gave me. Beliefs that cannot be foreclosed upon. Memories that won't be repossessed.

I don't look up. I don't feel watched. The Tower casts no shadow. I take my coat off, heading west. To Roncesvalles. Into the sun.

O

THE END

ACKNOWLEDGMENTS

The author wishes to acknowledge the following artists and their works, without which the composition of this novel would have been impossible.

- **Edward Hopper** (1882-1967): *Nighthawks (1942), Drug Store (1927), Night Shadows (1921).*
- **Hermann Hesse** (1877-1962): *Steppenwolf (1927)*
- **P.D. Ouspensky** (1878-1947): *The Symbolism of the Tarot (1913)*
- **Thomas Pynchon** (1937-): *The Crying of Lot 49 (1966), Gravity's Rainbow (1973), Inherent Vice (2009), Bleeding Edge (2013)*

AUTHOR'S NOTE

I wrote the first draft of this novel on my smartphone. During lunch breaks at the store where I worked. On long drives ferrying cargo around the province. Working outside in the frozen mud, breathing in the diesel fumes, wishing I was someone else.

I'm not complaining. I'm grateful. There's no substitute for being out there every day, alone with everybody, soaking in the chaos of the city, turning those days and nights into stories.

I'd like to write a follow-up. In fact, I'd like to write nine more William Keele novels. I hope to find a readership that makes it possible.

So if you enjoyed this book, please leave me a review. If you loved it, tell your friends. If you hated it, tell your enemies. Thank you for reading *Port Lands,* and for so generously supporting my work.

William
Keele
will
return
in
CROSS
TOWN.
Coming
soon
in
2024
from
Debtford
Press.

ABOUT THE AUTHOR

Tod Molloy is a freelance writer based in Toronto. His debut novel, *Port Lands*, was released on November 28th, 2022. Tod studied English Literature at the University of Toronto. He loves pancakes, the ocean, Modernism, Film Noir, Nicolas Cage, and creating mundane lists. His favourite author is Don DeLillo. In support of his *Hogtown Noir* series, Tod has launched *Too Late To Die Early,* an online blog for all things Noir. To keep up with Tod please visit todmolloy.com

ALSO BY TOD MOLLOY

PORT LANDS

CROSS TOWN (2024)

UNTITLED WILLIAM KEELE NOVEL (2025)

Manufactured by Amazon.ca
Bolton, ON

32955665R00136